The Running Woman

ALSO AVAILABLE BY PATRICIA CARLON

The Souvenir
The Whispering Wall

The Running Woman

Patricia Carlon

First published in Great Britain by Hodder and Stoughton

Copyright © 1966 by Patricia Carlon; first published in
the United States of America in 1998

Published by
Soho Press, Inc.
853 Broadway
New York, NY 10003

Library of Congress Cataloging-in-Publication Data

    Carlon, Patricia, 1927–
        The running woman / by Patricia Carlon.
            p.   cm.
        ISBN 1-56947-110-X
        I. Title.
    PR 9619.3.C37R86   1998
    823—dc21   97-16842
                                                       CIP

10 9 8 7 6 5 4 3 2 1

CHAPTER ONE

Larapinta. . . Running Water. . .

He thought of that and of the running water muddied and eddying after heavy rain. Yesterday it had probably carried tree branches, still leafed with autumn tints of red; possibly there'd been the soaked, grey-furred body of some tiny bush creature. . .

Definitely there'd been the girl. . .

The announcer's voice was flat, disinterestedly intoning, "She fell from the bridge."

His hand went out and the voice ceased, sound from outside filling the room again, but over the clash of boxes, the impatient passing of traffic, the clatter-chatter of voices right outside the window, the announcer's voice seemed echoing still, disinterestedly repeating over and over, "Her body was taken from the Larapinta. . ."

The second one, though the flat voice hadn't said so, and the newspapers hadn't reminded. They couldn't have forgotten though. Or had they, he wondered. Had time washed over those fifteen months, crowding them so with events, with people, with news and disasters that now no one but himself remembered that other morning, that other voice that echoed to him still across the months, "Her body was taken from the Larapinta. . ."

A door opened. Footsteps crossed to him. China rattled. He turned impatiently, almost angrily, at the girl's eager, "Did you hear? There's no cream this morning, sorry. But did you hear?" Her voice went on . . . cosily, he thought. That was the word. Cosy. A cosy talk of cream and chocolate biscuits, coffee and a choice item of news.

"Terrible, isn't it, Mr. Sturt?" She paused at the door to shake her head again. "Her body was taken from the Larapinta . . . a terrible thing, isn't it?"

The past, that other morning, the words he'd spoken then,

echoed in his croaked husk of sound, "Very terrible indeed."

. . .

Other voices echoed the three words that morning. In the echoes there was shock, pity, sympathy, even eager greed for a new item of gossip and speculation. Only in private thoughts was there remembrance so sharp and fear so great that hands had to be clenched to hold them still.

For Gabriel there was no emotion at all, except the vague disinterest that brushed lightly across thought and was gone almost at once—the news, like everything else in the past months, had a shimmering, unreal quality like a distantly-seen mirage.

Only the words Larapinta Creek touched her consciousness for a moment, then her hand went out and switched off the radio and everything the announcer had said was gone from memory.

Till the letter came.

She let the envelope lie there in her hand, considering it, knowing she didn't want to open it. The slanting "Gabriel Endicott" was like a strident summons, an intrudence on her privacy. The sealed envelope seemed almost a smug affront to it, because normal curiosity demanded it should be unsealed, and then normal courtesy demanded a physical and mental effort from her—a letter to be written, a phone call to be made, a visit to be extended.

She didn't want to make any effort at all. That was what annoyed Phil so much. He'd told her she was merely laying up trouble for herself; that she couldn't become a vegetable because of what had happened; that she had to get out and about and start living normally again. As though none of it had happened at all.

He hadn't said, as he might have done, "You knew Nicholas Endicott barely three months. You can't let three months' memories scar the whole of your life," and she hadn't been able to explain that the swiftness of everything, the meeting with Nicholas, their marriage, the quarrel and his death, had been so gaspingly fast none of it had seemed real; that she was still trying to catch up with everything that had happened, still trying to believe it had all happened . . . to herself.

6

Only the house was solid and real, and ugly.

She went on standing there in the garden, the letter in her hand, seeing the raw wood of the new paling fence that went round three sides of what would one day be the garden. Mellowed, greyed by time and the weather, it would have merged into the grey-greens of the tree-covered slopes further away and into the blue-grey of the autumn sky and gentled the harshness of the torn red earth that still lay in ridges and furrows inside it, but now its raw yellow tinge made the red earth the harsher, the uglier; fought with the new red brick of the low house, and flaunted itself in violent reflection in the huge glass windows.

Yet she knew it would one day be a beautiful place, a showplace, just as Nicholas had wanted. There was pleasure in standing there in the warm sunlight, lids half-closed over the grey-green of her eyes, picturing it as it would one day be—the red brick mellowed, the fence silvered by time and garlanded with creepers, the raw furrows disciplined to grass and flowers. But now . . . her eyes opened again . . . it, and the other raw fences and shining paint and new brickwork all through the district were . . . unreal.

As unreal as trying to put herself into the skin and thoughts of Gabriel Endicott, a stranger.

I'm still Gabriel Sturt she thought, and the thought was followed by another, I want to be still Gabriel Sturt. It was absurd, stupid, childish, a dozen other things, she knew, to wish that her name had never changed, even that she'd never met Nicholas at all.

The meeting had been Phil's doing, and Phil's kiss . . . her mouth thinned at the memory . . . had been the first doubt in her happiness with Nicholas. The second had been the house itself.

She remembered her amazement when Nicholas had brought her, straight after the wedding, to the vast new suburb rising out of bushland, and shown her the place, enthusing over it, pointing out details, telling her he had had it planned in his head for years.

She had asked in astonishment, "But didn't you ever think that the woman you eventually married might hate it?" and then had fallen silent in the face of his blank, narrow-eyed gaze.

"You don't like it," the accusation had flattened his normal deep, richly-vibrant voice. "Why?"

7

She had stammered and stuttered. Embarrassed. Dismayed. Because how could one say to a man that his dream was her nightmare—that her idea of a home was a mellow place, a small place, a place where one entertained a few friends at quiet dinners; not a showplace with a thirty-five foot living-room whose length of polished wood flooring cried out for crowded parties; where a vast aviary full of gaily-coloured budgerigars became part of the house, seen through fine silvered meshwork behind glass doors and heard through the whole house when the glass was moved back.

Nicholas had kept it back when he was home, so that the house was filled with birdsong. She had found it fascinating at first, irritating only as the days went on. Now she mostly kept the glass closed, but every time she looked at the fluttering birds she could remember Nicholas saying, "I couldn't live in a silent place," and her swift answering, "*I* couldn't live in perpetual noise."

There'd been so many differences between them that time had remorselessly pointed out. Even Nicholas's urgent drive for power and prestige clashed with her own shrinking from public life. The fact that he expected her to join committees with his own gay abandon and work on them tirelessly had at first openly amused her, and then later, frightened her, because in his startled blue gaze she had seen a new awareness, a strange questioning that echoed her own startled, "But how different we are!"

It had been the need of reassurance that had made her say to Phil one evening, "People say that opposites attract. Don't they? That opposites make the best marriage partners? Haven't I read that somewhere?"

Only when the question had been put did she wonder if the reason for the question had shown in her voice, but Phil, lounging against the mesh of the aviary, trying to tempt a cobalt-blue budgerigar with a slice of apple, seemed unconscious of the importance of what she had said.

"I don't know. I've read it somewhere, too, but I doubt it being true. Would you mate a tiger with a lamb, Angel?" He had turned fully then, a smile on his wide mouth that gave his sun-tanned face an oddly clownish look. She had remembered

8

vividly how often, when they'd been children, he'd been called Clown because of that wide mobile mouth and his great, dark blue that were almost black, strangely sorrowful-looking eyes. With maturity, the broadening and strengthening of face and stocky body, the old name had nearly gone, but her childish nickname of Angel had stayed with her.

Phil had called her that when he'd introduced her to Nicholas, and she could still remember looking into his blue eyes, seeing the startling contrast of black brows and hair so auburn the rich red had the glint of furnace-heat, and knowing a stab of dismay, something startlingly close to fear because a quite shattering degree of desire had torn at her heart and she had been afraid of what his half-laughing, "So this is the paragon Gabriel," implied.

She had wanted to know him better; had been afraid that already he knew her through and through, or thought he did, from Phil's talk of her, and that when he found her not a paragon at all his interest would be gone. Always, it had seemed to her, in her grown-up years, she had played a part with Phil, with other people, too, changing to please the wishes of people she loved and liked. Her mother had wanted a fairy-like daughter; her father a games-happy tomboy. Life had been a thing of constant turnings and twistings and suddenly, that night of meeting Nicholas, she had wanted someone, just for once, to accept her as she really was.

She had burst into aggressive, defensive speech, "Phil's been telling you a lot of nonsense, I expect. You shouldn't have listened to him. He's told you, I suppose, that I'm a sort of Florence Nightingale, doing good works when I could be sitting back attending fashion parades and first nights. That's nonsense. I don't like fashion parades or first nights, so it was sit and twiddle my thumbs or find some work to do. I'm not trained for anything and I started being a nursing aide simply because the advert was the first one in the positions vacant column. I don't think I'm even particularly good at it. I always seem to finish up doing the flowers and handing round the dinner trays. I haven't so much as soothed one fevered brow. In fact I fever them. I drop things, or tear them, or something disastrous. Sometimes," she had told him quite fiercely,

9

"I think whenever something's on its last legs the cry goes up 'Hand it to Sturt. She'll break it. And have to buy a new one'."

She had stopped then, red-faced from embarrassment, and fury at herself, and he'd said, "Phil certainly didn't tell me you were cross, or had a deeply suspicious mind. Come and tell me what you're really like."

It had been mad, she had realised later, that swift coming-together, that feeling of rightness, of being accepted at last, and later there'd never seemed time, or the need, for words, for question and answer, for discovering the true facets of each other's personality.

She had learned Nicholas owned a real estate firm in the fast-developing area that had once been her own home. The home and the land round it was gone now, caught up in the mad rush for new homes, as Phil's home had gone, too. In their time of their growing-up they'd shared childhood in homes not so far distant, in families that had intermingled with the warmth of second cousinship, and it had been Phil who had given her away at that wedding only three weeks after her first meeting with Nicholas.

He'd kissed her later and brought back the memory of several years before, when for a brief time they'd come together in a new relationship, thought life was perfect, and then parted because they'd found flaws in the perfection.

The kiss had had nothing of passion in it, yet it had reminded her, disconcertingly, of others given before, and suddenly she had thought, shockingly, "Phil's my type. Nicholas isn't," and the comparison had been there between the two men—between Nicholas's forceful personality and the quietness that had been her own and Phil's.

Had been, she had reminded herself.

Both of them had changed. Phil to a successful architect and to what more, she didn't know; herself to a woman of independent means, after her father's death, and to the sort of person who could be swept off her feet by Nick.

But a doubt, that there was a difference that might prove too great between herself and Nicholas, had suddenly been there, stayed there, and grown to anxiety, to reality, to arguments and bitter words, and her last, "I wish I'd never met you! I wish you were dead!"

How childish it sounded, in memory, but perhaps she'd never said that at all? None of those three months seemed real . . .

She closed her mind to it, ripping open the envelope, so that the small piece of paper inside fluttered to the ground. When she bent, picking it up, she found herself gazing at a portion of an advert that urged her to improve her memory with a course of twelve easy lessons.

For one horrible moment she felt violently sick, seeing it as a taunt that jeered, "Remember how you told him you wished he was dead, and he drove away in a rage . . . and they came and told you . . . he was dead? Remember. . . ?"

Then her shaking fingers had turned over the scrap of news-print, and sickness was lost in relief. Memory told her she had seen the tiny paragraph before, in the previous day's paper. Only the name of Larapinta Creek—the new suburb that had been carved out of the bushland round her old home, only a few miles from her present one in Paltara, had drawn her gaze to it at all.

It was only now, with the cutting in her hand, that she really thought about the girl. In spite of the sunlight she found herself touched by coldness, as though the waters of Larapinta . . . the Running Water that gave the place its name . . . had closed coldly about her own body. She thought of the creek as she'd seen it Monday evening on her visit there—swollen from heavy rain the previous week, ugly with debris of branches and cans, bottles and papers . . .

But some time on that Monday it had been uglier still. What time had it happened, she wondered. The cutting didn't say. The tiny print, the few words, seemed to shrink from detailing anything but the bare facts. "Girl drowns", said the heading. "Carol Zamia, 14, of Pitt Road, Larapinta, was drowned yesterday in Larapinta Creek. Her mother, Eileen Zamia, 40, told police that Carol was unable to swim."

She re-read the last paragraph. Re-read it again, and only then realised why the cutting had been sent. The pool, of course, she reflected. Nicholas's pet project. The one he would have finished but for driving off that night in a furious rage, and crashing the car, and . . .

She wasn't going to think of it. Steadily she forced her mind back to the dead girl, only thinking of Nicholas in connection with the plans for building an Olympic-standard swimming-pool in the district before the next summer. Part of his argument had been that the creek was almost empty of water in summer, and unsafe for swimming at any time, but that children and adults, too, were tempted into it.

So someone had seen the small paragraph and snipped it out, thinking possibly the girl's death could be used as campaign propaganda. There was something faintly distasteful in the idea, even while she admitted the sense of it. It would be for Phil to decide anyway, she reflected. Not herself. Even though he'd forced her willy-nilly to join the committee, when he'd stepped into Nicholas's shoes as head of it.

"You can't sit here and brood," he'd told her bluntly. "And you might as well be useful. This pool idea was Nick's right from the beginning. Don't you want to be part of the building and finishing of it?"

Useless to say she didn't; impossible to say that their last quarrel had been about the swimming-pool, about her refusal to give generously of her own money to the funds for it. She had thought her argument for refusal was good—that her money wasn't end-less—that there'd be another fund after the pool one, and others after that, and they'd be expected to give just as generously to them all. Nicholas had only raged, talked of crossing bridges when she came to them, told her . . .

She closed her mind on it again, abruptly went inside, reaching for the morning paper, thinking there could be more details she could clip ready for Phil to go over.

But in the small announcement on the third page there was nothing to interest him. Only a puzzle.

"Police are anxious," she frowned over the words, "to interview a woman seen running from Larapinta Creek Bridge on Monday evening. It is believed she may have seen Carol Zamia, 14, fall from the bridge after the girl caught the heel of her shoe in the bridge planks. The woman is described as young, fair-haired and wearing a white dress."

Why run away? The question probed at Gabriel's thoughts, to be instantly answered by a rueful, "Of course, she couldn't swim either, poor thing. She had to try and find help."

Evidently though she'd never found it. She'd never come back again. Why not?

How odd, she reflected. Why hadn't she returned? She must have seen the girl fall and then . . .

Suddenly she could think only that if she herself had seen the girl fall she wouldn't have been able to help—she'd have had to run, desperately, through the evening, to find someone else. Where would she have gone? Memory dwelt on the district round the creek, as she'd seen it Monday. She would have raced for the houses, she decided. It would have been natural to turn down-hill, not up towards the ridge, to the occupied places there. But the houses downhill weren't occupied. As yet they were still only frames of future houses. So no help there. She'd have had to turn back, to the ridge, or go on running along the creek path, hoping to find someone. She'd probably have run on and on, not seeing anyone, till finally she reached the town . . .

Why hadn't she roused a rescue party then?

She'd been so engrossed in the mental picture of the child fall-ing; the woman's distraught, anguished running, that could have echoed her own actions in a similar case, that she hadn't heard anything, but suddenly the room was filling with the sound of birds. The paper fell from her hands as she whirled round, staring, memory crowding in on her, of other times she'd been startled when Nicholas had come softly home, and suddenly the birdsong had filled the house.

Only this time it was Phil who was smiling at her.

Suddenly she was running to him, clinging to him. The words were out before she had time to calm down. "There was a child drowned! Phil, I couldn't have saved her. Do you realise that?"

His arms had started to tighten round her. Now they loosened again. He held her at arm's length. He said slowly, "Someone drowned? You were there?"

"No," impatience sharpened her voice. She grudged the time wasted on explanations; she wanted immediate comfort for the shock that had seared at her mind. She said, "I was reading in the paper about the girl. She fell into the Larapinta and she drowned because she couldn't swim. And I realised I couldn't have saved her, because I can't swim either."

His hands, on her shoulders, gave her a little shake. "Still?"

She grimaced, half in self-disgust. He said slowly, absently, "You should have learned long ago. Oh I know all about that rheumatic odd-job you had, but all that cotton wool your fond mamma coddled round you wasn't necessary." In the too-casual way he always introduced Nick's name into things he added, "What did Nick have to say about it?"

"Nothing. He didn't know." She turned away. She didn't want to think of the way Nicholas might have looked at her in impatient disgust if he'd known. She said rapidly, "I think the parents kept on insisting I was fragile just to keep me away from dipping my toes in the creek. Mother was certain, you know, that every wog under the sun lurked at the bottom and . . . I wonder —you'd think, wouldn't you, this girl's family would have made her stay away from the creek when she couldn't swim. Anyway, why couldn't she? Isn't swimming compulsory at school these days, or . . . but, of course, there was no pool for swimming lessons! Phil, there's a splendid piece of propaganda . . ."

He shook his head. "She had her chance to learn two summers ago. Oh yes, I know all about it. Quite a few people have rung me about it, but . . . there were free lessons at a pool fifteen miles away last year, and free buses as well for the kids. Carol Zamia refused to go. She was fat and said the other kids were poison to her when she trotted out in swimming togs. I'm afraid that's argument for nothing but dieting," he mocked gently.

"Poor Carol," she said, but her thoughts had drifted back to the woman in white.

It was a cold shock at first, and then only a matter of interest, when she suddenly remembered that on the Monday she had worn a cream jersey suit. And she was fair-haired. And young. She'd been near the creek in the evening, too.

The remembrance came, shocked her and retreated under the other remembrance that she hadn't been near the bridge and that at no time at all had she been running.

CHAPTER TWO

On Thursday morning there were two cuttings in the white envelope with the slanted "Gabriel Endicott" across the front. One was the paragraph about the running woman. She barely glanced at it. The vision of the woman in white, running frantically through the evening, past half-built houses, was a nagging irritation that refused to go away.

The other cutting was larger, from an evening paper, she realised, and suddenly for her Carol Zamia was no longer just a name. The printed photograph was blurred, and Carol stared out from it with half-closed eyes, apparently against the glare of the sun. There was nothing of prettiness in the round heavy features, the pouting mouth and snub, almost flattened nose, with a dark fringe of hair almost meeting the straight thick bars of eyebrows, but one day she might, Gabriel thought, have been what people called a distinguished-looking woman.

The printing below the photograph purported to be an interview with Mrs. Zamia. Whether the woman had lied, or the reporter had thought it politic to gloss over the real reason for Carol's inability to swim, it told the world that Carol had been delicate.

Gabriel, reading on, reflected that probably most of it was lies, or half-truths. If it was to be believed, Carol Zamia had been a paragon of all virtues, devoted to her family, and working on Saturday mornings to help with family finances, as well as studying hard at school. "She wanted to be a nurse," Mrs. Zamia was reported to have said. "She just loved helping people. One of her teachers had been off school sick and I think Carol was taking her flowers when she fell that way.'

There was something infinitely pathetic in the idea of the girl and the little posy of flowers, falling together. Gabriel, reading the cutting again, reflected that the flowers though were probably the cause of the accident. Memory reminded her that the bridge was merely a strip of planks, with a railing on one side only, sufficient for crossing the trickle of water that usually ran there beneath it. But on the Monday evening with the creek swollen, the water would have been very near the planks. She could easily picture Carol, the heel of her shoe caught, her arms burdened with flowers, giving a wrench to her foot, and the shoe staying fixed, but her foot sliding free and toppling her over. Without the flowers she would probably have caught at the railing before wrenching at the shoe.

She crumpled the cuttings, letting them fall into the mound of leaves and rubbish she had been raking together when the post had come. Bending, she set a match to it, standing there smelling the tang of burning gum leaves above the smoke.

Whoever had sent the cuttings, she reflected, hadn't known the true reason why Carol couldn't swim. She—or he—evidently thought the committee would be able to make fuel for their plans out of the drowning of a girl who was partly the family bread-winner.

When she turned from the bonfire the whole thing was almost forgotten. The autumn day's warmth was a sweet pleasure, the gum-leaf smoke another; even the red furrows and weals in the earth didn't flick her nerves as much as usual. She was actually reluctant to go inside when the phone rang and she let the ringing go on and on, hoping that whoever it was would simply give up, but the persistence of the caller finally outmatched her resistance.

She jerked, almost angrily in her resentment, "Who?" and then asked, "Did you say . . . Fred Zamia . . . *Zamia*?"

"Yes. That Mrs. Endicott?"

"Mrs. Endicott," she echoed, surprise dulling her wits, then said swiftly, "Of course it is," nearly adding in resentment, "Don't you know I live alone?"

But the man was saying, "You'll remember my wife?"

Blankness settled down on her mind. "Why no. I'm sorry. I don't." She groped hazily in memory, but there was only blankness. She was certain she had never before heard the name Zamia before reading about Carol.

"Eileen Austin that was, Mrs. Endicott. I'm sure you'll remember now, eh?"

"But I don't . . . why of course!" But even while she tried to instil pleased remembrance into her voice she was still groping for remembrance. Eileen Austin had been someone of . . . surely fifteen years before? When she had been only a child. Not more than ten. And Phil had been . . . fourteen. It was that fact that brought the name into full focus. Gabriel's parents had been alive then and had gone away for a month. Gabriel herself had gone to Phil's home, and there had been a woman who came in each week to do the washing and ironing. Two days of the week. For the month Gabriel had been there. Little enough to remember somebody by. She wouldn't have remembered at all, except for Phil's fourteenth birthday having fallen in that month. Eileen Austin had come to help with the party. Memory was growing stronger as she went on standing there, remembering the screams, Eileen's blood-stained arm after she'd fallen on a knife. There'd been a horrible excitement about the day that now she could clearly remember. She said into the phone, "Eileen Austin, of course. I never realised . . ." then stopped, wondering why Phil hadn't mentioned the fact when they'd talked of the girl's death; wondering if it had been the woman who'd sent the cuttings.

The question was answered when the voice asked, "You get the cuttings, Mrs Endicott? Eileen said maybe you didn't. As you haven't done anything."

Gabriel stared helplessly at the wall. What had she been expected to do, she wondered uneasily? Start a sensation, an uproar? Turn the dead girl into a kind of martyr to there being no swimming pool?

She said slowly, "I had the cuttings. The last two arrived here only an hour ago. We have a late delivery here,' she prattled on, waiting for him to give her a lead as to what they expected.

But all he said was, "I didn't think of that. We get ours about nine."

"Ours is late," she babbled, "nearly one o'clock usually."

"Ah." The sound was heavy. Then he said slowly, "Then I guess you mean to come on out this afternoon, eh?"

18

"This . . ." her mind went blank again. Was she expected to go and console the woman on the strength of eight or nine meetings fifteen years ago, she wondered in astonishment. It was incredible. But of course, she realised, impatient now with her own stupidity, it was the pool. They expected her to go out and discuss the idea of using Carol's death in publicity. There was a vague wonderment in her mind that they could have the strength of purpose to write and ring and want her to go; to face the publicity; the constant reminder of the girl's death.

When Nick had died, she reflected, and relived again the sick horror of those after-days, she had only wanted to be left alone, not even to mention his name. But of course, memory probed remorselessly, the Zamias hadn't quarrelled with Carol, hadn't wished her dead, hadn't . . .

I'm not going to think about it, she told herself sharply. I won't. And because the only way to do that was to think of something else, to drown thought completely in some other action, she said, "Of course I'll come on out, Mr. Zamia, if you like. Would Mrs. Zamia be home at . . . three? Four?"

"We're both home," the words came heavily. "They gave me time off the job, when they knew."

"Oh yes of course. They would."

Now she was committed to going she shrank from it. What on earth had made her be such a fool as to agree, she thought resentfully. But now she had to go, had to face the woman. There'd be tears for a certainty, and she doubted that the heavy-voiced man would be of any help. She could picture herself seated in some half-lit living-room, striving to make conversation, trying not to hurt their feelings—the way people had come to the Endicott house when they'd known about Nick, to murmur soothing platitudes, to talk of her great loss . . .

"So if you'd come at three," the words came across her thoughts, "We'd both be here. I'll tell Eileen to expect you, eh?"

. . .

Pitt Road, she found, was part of a housing commission estate, where the small fenced-in homes were barrack-like either side the long, arrow-straight road. Some time in the future, when the now-tiny, stick-like trees along the footpaths came to maturity, and when gardens had blossomed in the small front yards, it would be a pleasant enough area. Now it was dulled by uniformity, newness, and too many of the front gardens were merely earth dumps for scattering of toys, though there wasn't a child to be seen.

She reflected that at that hour harrassed women would probably be recovering their breath from the morning hours, with pre-schoolers asleep and older children not yet out of school. Probably later on there would be life in abundance, but now the only person in sight was an elderly woman, slippered feet splayed, head hidden in an absurd blue pixie hat, face ruminative, blank, as she held a hose turned on a tiny garden where a terra-cotta elf leered per-petually at the roadway.

Gabriel's destination was the next house. Here was raw earth, a battered tricycle and two discarded dolls left on the concreted path-way. The woman with the hose didn't look round as Gabriel went up the path, but the house door opened long before she reached it.

The sun was in Gabriel's eyes. The figure awaiting her was blurred, featureless, till she stepped on to the porch. There was no recognition in her thoughts as she ventured a half-smile. For all her groping through memory, she had been unable to form a clear picture of the Eileen Austin of fifteen years before. Now there was still no recognition in her, only acknowledgement that from her mother Carol must have gained her pouting mouth and small, almost flattened nose, but here the face was longer, the chin pinched and pointed, the head with its gingery-blonde hair small and narrow.

And there was a baby expected. Gabriel was abruptly conscious that the woman's stance—heavy body seemed to thrust forwards on the stick-thin legs that were slightly bowed, as though incapable of bearing the weight of pregnancy—was aggressive, pointedly making the visitor aware of its burden.

Was it a bid for extra sympathy? Gabriel pondered the point as she walked the last few steps to the porch. Or Pride in her con-dition, Pride with a capital P, she thought in wry amusement—

the sort of pride many pregnant women showed in front of those who were childless?

Then Eileen Zamia said, "Hello, Gabriel."

The sympathy in Gabriel was lost in startlingly sharp annoyance. She stopped in mid-step, knowing that she resented, quite definitely and angrily, the woman's use of her christian name. She told herself that it was absurd to feel that way; that the majority of people used christian names as a matter of course; but there was unease in her mind as she murmured "Mrs. Zamia?" because the woman's tone, she was quite sure, hadn't been a mere friendly remembrance, but something more; a determination to trade on the past, to impose on Gabriel's sympathy . . .

For what? Gabriel wondered.

The woman lifted her right hand, puffed almost urgently on the cigarette between her fingers, blow a cloud of smoke into the air between them and said, "A'course you wouldn't remember me well, but the Sturts was my last job before I married Fred, and it ended so funny, if you know what I mean." She stood back. "Come on in. I never went back after the accident, you know. It shook me up and my arm turned nasty. A'course there was the compensation they paid me for being laid up like that. Come on into the sitting-room."

Gabriel followed silently. The house smelled of furniture polish and cigarette smoke and stale air. She was hardly conscious of it. She was reflecting that she had never wondered about Eileen Austin's accident; whether the arm had healed or not. She didn't even remember any family discussion about it, or the compensation that had evidently been paid out.

Eileen Zamia was saying, "Mrs. Sturt was always a good sort. I sent flowers to the funeral, you know. Couldn't go. I was expecting Mark then. That's our eldest boy. A'course you wouldn't know, Gabriel, but I'm expecting my eighth. Or rather," she suddenly swung round from altering the flow of light from the venetian blinds over the windows, to stand, aggressively still, in the crowded little room, "now it'll mean we have seven again. Now Carol's gone, a'course."

The hot, airless little room, the woman's thin, thrusting voice,

21

the silent figure of Fred Zamia, who had been standing by the windows when the two women had come in, unnerved Gabriel.

She said hurriedly, "I was most terribly sorry, Mrs. Zamia. I . . ."

"Words," the heavy sound seemed to thud into the airless little space round them, "are easy."

Gabriel turned slightly, gazing at him, helpless under a force that she realised now, in shocked astonishment, was hostility.

Remembering the photo in the cutting, she could see where Carol had gained her heavy features and thick bars of brows. Fred Zamia's sun-reddened face was heavy, too, with down-drooping mouth, the big head, with its coarse, springy, greying dark hair, set so low on the thick neck he seemed perpetually hunched down on to his broad shoulders.

Annoyance touched her again. Annoyance for the contemptuous brushing aside of her stammered words, and for her own uneasiness.

She drew a deep breath. She wasn't going to wait for them to mention the swimming-pool, she knew. She was going to speak her condolences, and then go, refusing to allow the woman to dwell on the supposed intimacy of the past, refusing to question that shocking hostility.

Deliberately, without waiting to be asked, she sat down in one of the rust-coloured chairs. It was hard, uncomfortable, unresisting against the weight of her body.

Looking up at them she said, "As I was saying, I was terribly sorry about Carol. It was a dreadful thing. It . . ."

"You're right there." Fred Zamia nodded his big head. "What'd be more dreadful than leaving a bit of a kid to drown?"

"Leaving . . . you mean the running woman, but . . ." she stopped, that mental picture of the woman running desperately through the evening nagging at her again.

Why hadn't the woman gone back?

It was a question unanswerable. She started to say so, then said sharply, "But of course! She didn't see Carol fall. She couldn't have. She must have seen her later—floating . . ." she stopped.

What am I saying? She asked herself that in desperation. How

22

dare I say such a thing? To this woman? Even though they're so hostile . . . and why are they? How could I say that, making them picture her moving sluggishly, drowned eyes blank . . .

She began again stumblingly, "She came along later. Perhaps she thought it was one of . . . well, these dreadful assault cases. She could have been terrified. Don't you think that? Not wanting to be involved. She might have thought of the police, and newspapers, an inquest, even a trial . . ."

Eileen Zamia was busily lighting a new cigarette from the stub of the old one.

"The police say it was maybe like that. But a'course you'd know better than them. Or us. The police say it was that or someone slapped her off, and then ran off ashamed. Which was it, Gabriel? We know it was you ran off and left her anyway."

CHAPTER THREE

Eileen Zamia said, into the hot silence, "I remembered right off 'bout you not swimming. I remembered the fuss there was 'bout that party, with young Phil wanting a river picnic and Mrs. Sturt crying off because of you, Gabriel. You couldn't swim. And you still can't. I asked Phil. He sent flowers, you know. I've kept up with them all—Christmas cards and that, if you know what I mean. And he sent flowers. He was always thoughtful that way, even as a little fellow. Like Mrs. Sturt was. And when I heard . . . well, see I rang Phil. I told him Fred'n me appreciate the flowers and all that and I'd been thinking of you—I saw your picture in the local papers a few weeks back. You'd just come back from your honeymoon—Mrs. Nicholas Endicott, it said . . . Gabriel Sturt that was, see. I said that to Phil and I said, with Carol in mind a'course, 'Can Gabriel swim yet, Phil?' and he said, 'My God, no! I've just remembered that.' He sounded real startled, if you know what I mean, and then he said something like Carol brought it home to him about the like of you not being safe . . .

"Well anyway, there it was. So I guessed what happened. And then a'course you didn't know those houses were just going up, did you, Gabriel? It'd need a stranger round here to take that way from the creek to look for help. I said so to Fred. Locals'd know to make for the ridge right off, but you . . . you went away from here when your house got sold, didn't you? And I guess you were too busy ever to look at Larapinta till just last Monday . . . why'd you come anyway?"

The words were out before she had time to think; before she realised she should have denied being near the place, to put an end to the ridiculous accusation. She said rapidly, "I was this way and I suddenly thought I had time to look at the old place . . . I just left the bus and walked and . . ." she stopped.

Eileen Zamia was nodding. "I guessed it'd be some way like that.

But why?" her voice was shriller, accusing, "didn't you remember the bridge was only six feet over the creek bed? There's that little red tag on the edge of the rail even now. Height six feet, it says. You must've remembered. Young Phil put that there one winter when everyone was asking one another how high the creek was after some rain. Six feet over the bed it is. He must've told you, Gabriel . . ."

He had, Gabriel remembered with startling clarity. She had been present herself, held firmly by Phil's elder sister, away from the water, when Phil had screwed the neatly-made sign to the railings of the bridge.

Eileen Zamia went on in the same excited voice, "And the water wasn't over the bridge Monday. It was a good foot below. You must've seen that, Gabriel. You could've stood up in it—you must be all of five foot eight. But Carol couldn't. She wasn't five foot even. The water was over her head, but if you'd had the guts . . . the simple guts . . . to jump in you could've stayed on your feet, dragged her out and maybe got her round in time. Only you didn't, Gabriel. You just ran, didn't you," and again the words were a statement, not a question.

Fred Zamia coughed, raspingly.

It was the sound that jerked Gabriel from frozen stillness, from shock and something close to terror. She said, the words rushing out in anger and fright, "This is ridiculous! What are you trying to do? I wasn't near Carol. I wasn't . . ."

"You were at the creek. You said so. Mark says so." Fred Zamia was bending slightly forward, as though he wanted to inspect her closely.

"Mark?" she managed.

"Our eldest boy. Ten and a half, Gabriel, but a'course you weren't to know he was mine, were you, but he recognised you right off. I showed him that picture of you, see, and told him about you and he remembered. And he told us when he came home. Before we knew 'bout Carol that was. 'Mum,' he says, 'I met that Gabriel of yours down by the creek. Wearing a white suit. Real nice she looked.'"

Gabriel stood up. She said violently, "if he says I was running

25

from the bridge he's lying! I wasn't near the bridge. I'm not staying here to be . . ."

"Why'd you come?" Fred Zamia was still peering at her, "if it wasn't you? If you hadn't caught on we knew? I asked whyn't you done anything and you said the last letter'd just come. Didn't you, eh? And you said you'd come out to see us."

Gabriel tried to think. Clearly now she remembered her stammered, "we have a late delivery . . . the last two arrived here only an hour ago" . . . and one, she remembered, had been the cutting with the story of the running woman. And the Zamias had been expecting her to go straight and see them . . .

Why?

She gazed at them almost wonderingly. In a deadened voice she said, "I was certainly near the creek. I never went near the bridge I assure you. And as for this story . . . you, of course," she strove to make her tone almost indulgent, "know your son better than I do, but does he make up stories? Invent things? Put two and two together—like a woman by the creek and his sister dying— and make a hundred and six? Really, Mrs. Zamia," in spite of herself her voice began to shake under the stimulus of anger and shock, "this is quite abominable, and you must realise it is. I came here on the strength of vague acquaintance with you years ago. I thought you wanted . . . that you thought Carol's death could help the publicity for the swimming-pool. If I'd realised . . ." she brushed her hand across her face. It was wet, she realised, as though she'd been running, performing some terrible exertion. She finished, "I advise you to speak seriously to . . . Mark? That's his name, isn't it? He's invented . . ."

"Wasn't Mark." Fred Zamia was shaking his head. "Wasn't Mark said it."

Eileen Zamia broke in quickly, "It was Mark told us who you were, recognising you, see. But it was Mrs. Buchanan up on the ridge who saw you running that way. You came rushing out of those trees near the bridge. She told the police."

It wasn't possible.

Gabriel felt she had spoken the words aloud, but the two faces turned to hers were only blank, watchful. She wanted to speak, to assure them that Mrs. Buchanan was lying, too, even while her thoughts were turning frantically in the trap that had spread out in front of her.

Two people lying? That wasn't possible either. Two young, fair-haired women in white, walking by the creek at the same time? That was hardly credible either. And white wasn't a normal colour for wearing for a ramble near the creek. Her jersey suit had been put on for a visit to the city. It had been impulse that had made her leave the bus in Larapinta and walk down to the creek to see how much things had altered.

She asked, and her voice seemed to herself to be grating with harshness, with anger, "Who is Mrs. Buchanan? How did she see . . . ?"

"She lives in one of the houses on the ridge. The one with the pink door, Gabriel." Eileen Zamia drew in on her cigarette jerkily. "She's one of these foreigners," her pouting mouth pursed. "There's a lot of them round here now. We try not to mix, a'course, but Carol had a sort of craze on this Lisa Buchanan. She was at that stage, if you know what I mean. She met Mrs. B. somewhere and was full of her for a bit, then it fizzled out, but that's how we know she's one of these Germans. Came on out after the war and married one of us. . ." her pursed mouth showed her disapproval, the gulf she had set between migrants and home-grown stock . . . "then he died. So she's a widow. Up there by herself and she's got this telescope thing. Spends her days sticky-beaking if you ask me. These foreigners're all the same—nosey as all get out. Anyway she was up there Monday watching."

Carefully she crushed the cigarette out in a glass ashtray on the shelf over the tiny electric fire.

"She saw you running like crazy, Gabriel. It got her curious, a'course. She thought for a bit maybe a man'd been playing the fool, but no one followed you. Then she thought snakes. The creek rising's flooded dozens of them out of holes—but a'course you'd know the way they come out after rain. So she got that big dog of hers and a stick and pussy-footed down."

She was gazing down at the cold bars of the electric fire, her voice flat, expressionless, as she added, "the dog saw our Carol

27

and Mrs. Buchanan and him waded in and pulled her out. It was too late, but."

She turned, stretched, placing the palms of her hands in the small of her back, arching her body.

Gabriel was sure it wasn't to ease tiredness. It was another agressive pointing up of her swollen body.

But why?

The woman was saying, "But it mightn't've been, if you'd gone on and got help, Gabriel. Carol half came round and then . . . she died. So you see it wouldn't have been too late perhaps. The police say someone could have slapped her off and never realised she couldn't swim, but they think it more likely she just tripped and this woman came along later. Only wouldn't you think she'd have jumped in and dragged her out and tried to get her round, like Mrs. B? Only this one didn't. What Fred'n me think happened is that you saw her fall all right, but you couldn't do a thing. And you thought she'd be able to help herself. And then . . you realised she couldn't, didn't you, and you fled for those houses. That's when Mrs. B saw you. But you couldn't find anyone and we bet you hared off down the path, scared out of your wits. That's when Mrs. B came down. And then, when you'd run away, you got desperate, and decided to turn back. You got back to the creek and you saw Mrs. B there and saw her with Carol and Carol looking as though she'd gone and you were frightened. That's when you started thinking of police and newspapers and inquests and things and how it was going to look with you admitting you couldn't swim, hadn't tried to get her out. And we bet you remembered the tag on the bridge then, and thought people might say you'd known but been too cowardly . . . well you sneaked off behind Mrs. B's back, didn't you? Oh, it adds up right enough. But if you'd only gone forwards you could have raced off for help while she kept working on Carol. As it was she had to leave her and get help on her own. There was a whole long delay till she got back and the ambulance and all came."

Gabriel stood up. She asked, horrified at the shrillness of her voice, "Why did you get me here? To give yourselves some sort of crazy revenge by . . . by taunting me . . . by telling me you're going to the police now and that soon . . ."

She saw the two of them glance at each other. Then the woman shook her head. "That's not it at all, Gabriel. Fred'n me aren't going to tell. If the police got hold of your name and you not being able to swim, and maybe too late remembering about that tag on the bridge . . . well, we're swearing Mark to secrecy. And Fred'n me're going to keep quiet, too."

And am I supposed to be grateful, she wondered numbly. Am I supposed to thank them and crawl out the doorway?

She stood up violently. "There's not a word of it that's true. Except . . . I was by the creek. I admit that. And . . . if this boy recognised me he must have known where I was going . . ."

"Towards the bridge, Gabriel."

She tried to remember. Had there been a child? Dimly she could now remember a small boy on the creek bank. Just sitting there. It was true, too, that she'd been going past the houses, towards the bridge. The sunset was being swallowed up in a great bank of black cloud in the west, and the whole place had turned suddenly chill and thoroughly unpleasant.

But where had the boy been when she'd turned back. She couldn't place him in any mental picture of that journey back. She could see the sky and the creek . . . nothing more, excepting the path.

She said, "I wasn't near the bridge. I didn't know about Carol."

"People would say you did. Would you say so?"

She turned in the doorway, licking at dry lips. "Just what do you want me to do?" In furious anger she abruptly raged, "If you think I'm now going to thank you and crawl to you; beg for your silence . . ."

"Why not sit down, Gabriel? I'll make us a cuppa a bit later on." The solicitude was mocking. "Don't panic. Fred and me wouldn't have things ruined for you. After all you've got to go on living here. And working here too, so I've heard. Or isn't that so? Are you thinking of moving on?"

She knows, Gabriel thought, and the upsurge of fury came and died down all in a moment, under the realisation that of course the whole district must know. After Nick's death there'd been such a crowd of creditors waving papers under her nose, ringing her, writing to her, that the extent of Nick's debts must be known everywhere. Phil had tried to channel them away from her at first; had told her to turn it all over to Nick's solicitors; had wanted her to keep her shares and her income intact. Only when he had realised that selling everything would mean she owned Nick's business outright and would have to take a personal interest in it because the temporary manager wouldn't stay for long, had he let her go ahead.

She hadn't admitted to him her shares had been sold at a loss. She hadn't cared that finally all she owned was Nick's dream house and the business. There'd been even a vague comfort in the knowledge that when she was over the shock there'd be work to keep her occupied; a settled niche in the world for her to occupy. There'd been a salving of conscience too in the saving of Nick's home and business. Absurd really, she had told herself, but there was still comfort in the knowledge that even if she had disappointed him, sent him on that last furious ride, she had kept his dreams intact.

But now she was completely tied to the district. She had to live there. Earn her living there. Even if she tried to sell both house and business there'd be month and months . . .

She imagined the people she knew listening to the story. Would they believe that two people were wrong? Or would they believe, knowing she couldn't swim, that it was all true?

She thought of the whispers, the sidelong glances, the quiet dropping of herself from invitations, from committees . . . people shunning the firm simply because she, Gabriel Endicott, owned it. People were hardest on others for the very sins they might have committed themselves. Let everyone say she'd sneaked away from the possibility of publicity, thinking only of herself, not the girl, and wagging tongues would have a field day.

She said dully, "It's nothing to do with me. Nothing."

Eileen Zamia might have been speaking to a child.

"Don't be silly now. Fred'n me are going to help you. All we can. We thought as a sort of return you might be willing to help us. We're in a rare pickle. You know Carol was a sort of bread-winner here as well as Fred? Me . . ." she held her hands each side her swollen body, "well a'course I can't work. And Fred's pay's not going to stretch for all the things we just got to have. Carol had a Saturday job and did a bit of baby-sitting too. And she helped us out. She couldn't leave school yet, but what she did earn was . . . well, we *needed* it, Gabriel. Even more now, with this new one due in seven weeks. Twenty-four dollars a month regular cash Carol brought in."

Gabriel gazed blankly back. The words, the insinuation, hardly penetrated her thoughts. She was still thinking of Nick's firm going downhill; of people staring, whispering . . .

She said, "Mrs. Zamia, there are laws against this sort of thing. I'm not sure if it's called libel or slander, but it's one or the other. Your story's impossible. Quite untrue."

"Would other people say so?"

The panic was back, stifling her in the hot, airless room.

Fred Zamia said heavily, "We lost our girl and . . ."

"Twenty-four dollars a month, regular!" The bitter mockery was spat out before she'd had time to think. Then she said defiantly, "This is blackmail."

"Don't be silly." The voice was as flat as her own. "We've only told you how we're placed, what a pickle we're in with Carol gone like that. You don't have to help us. You can go right away and forgot everything we've said. Can't she, Fred?"

And then you'll tell . . .

The words, unspoken, were a mocking clamour in thought, together with the questions: What will everyone say? And believe? And do?

CHAPTER FOUR

The house had a pink door, as Eileen Zamia had said. It was small, solid, of fibro on brick foundations and a big flame tree glorified the front of the garden. As Gabriel hesitated by the gate a woman came from the side of the house, wheeling a barrow. Her hands were gloved, and she held the rake from the barrow expertly, working among the fallen leaves with long sweeps, while Gabriel continued standing there, unnoticed.

She called at last, huskily, "Mrs. Buchanan?" and the woman turned.

"Yes?"

It was only standing there that Gabriel realised she had given no thought as to what she was going to say. It was impossible to say now, "Mrs. Buchanan, am I the woman you saw running from the bridge on Monday?" without giving herself away.

The elder woman was coming towards her, expectant. Like her house she was small and neat, slim-figured, youthful-looking. It was only as she approached that Gabriel realised distance had gilded with kindness. The woman's face was lined, her small mouth tight, her brows pencilled in in thick strokes.

But her voice and smile were both pleasant when she said, "I'm Lisa Buchanan. You want me?"

"I'm intruding . . . you're busy," Gabriel began helplessly, still groping for words, then suddenly they were there on the tip of her tongue. They spilled out eagerly, "Mrs. Buchanan, I'm Gabriel Endicott. You've heard of my husband? Haven't you?" She pressed. "He . . ."

"Yes?" There was interest now in the waiting face.

"I'm carrying . . . trying to carry . . . on with his work. The pool, you know. When I heard about Carol Zamia dying I thought . . ."

A little grimace marred the woman's expression. Her big dark eyes grew wary. She said, still pleasantly, but quite definitely, "I am very tired of that subject. It was . . . terrible. For Carol. For me, also. You understand?"

"Oh I do, indeed. You were the one who found her."

"More. I pulled her from the water. I and Bruno. He is my dog, you understand? I also tried, very hard—terribly hard—to bring her round."

Gabriel saw that the gloved hands were shaking. The woman's gaze followed hers. With a frown she said, "I am still shocked. It distresses me very much to speak of it all."

Her gaze turned again to Gabriel's face. It said, quite plainly, please go away.

Gabriel ignored it. At the risk of appearing boorish, or angering the elder woman, she had to learn all she could. She pressed, "Mrs. Buchanan, it distresses me terribly, too. That's why I came. You see, Carol couldn't swim. If only she'd been able to this would never have happened. It's exactly to stop this sort of tragedy that we need the pool."

She knew now exactly what she was going to say. Her only fear was that the woman might agree to her first suggestion, but watching the shaking hands she was fairly sure she wouldn't.

"I was wondering, Mrs. Buchanan, if you'd address a district meeting, and tell just what happened—how you dived in and dragged Carol out and so on. You see, there's a big migrant population in this district. They're not really interested in swimming. Most of them can't swim themselves. So they're indifferent to our plans. But I want them to hear you and then I want them to ask what *they'd* do faced with the same thing—a tragedy happening to someone they loved, perhaps. I want to start them thinking, realising we need this pool desperately . . . if we have them clamouring for swimming lessons for themselves and their children it will be a big help."

The woman's gaze was abstracted. Then she shook her head. "My nerves—that's the excuse of the weak, the cowardly? I can't help it. The fact is, I could never do it. To stand on a platform . . . no! Yet, of course, you are right. We . . . I was once a German, Mrs. Endicott, do you realise?" her smile was gentle. "We tend to stand so much aloof. I myself swim like a mermaid . . ." abruptly she chuckled, "an aged mermaid, you think? But I could not . . ."

"Then would you tell me your story so I could make it into a statement?"

"Yes." Her eyes lit up again. "Of course. Gladly. You would like to come in now?"

She led the way into a front room of the house. To Gabriel's eyes it was almost stark in its simplicity—bare polished wood floors, the simplest, most necessary of furniture. But close to the window was a stand, a telescope.

"I was seated here." She patted the stand.

Gabriel went to her side, bending. Lisa Buchanan pushed forward one of the straight-backed wooden chairs, so that it touched the back of the girl's knees. Seated, suddenly excited, Gabriel adjusted the lens . . . and a faint cry broke from her lips.

The trees that hid the bridge were suddenly leaping forward. The narrow track of path was clear too. The running woman, she realised eagerly, must have stood out plainly enough.

And Lisa Buchanan had shown no signs of recognising her visitor.

There was sweet relief in that realisation. She saw the tiny huddle of half-built houses, asked, "You saw the woman running away? Who was she?"

"Poor feeble creature . . . I do not know."

"Poor?" She turned.

"What else would you call her? A creature who thinks only of inconvenience to herself. It reminds me of that other case—the man who tried to commit suicide and the policeman who rushed to restrain him calling for help to a passer-by and that man . . . he walked past with averted face, calling back, 'It's not my business, mate.'" She grimaced. "That is the twin brother of this woman." She looked up almost belligerently, "You think it is different—that his action was far worse because he could have helped? That perhaps the man could have died . . . all because of his averted face? But it was the same here. The girl wasn't dead. She stirred, but I knew she was going. I had to decide—stay and perhaps some-

34

how I will bring her right round. I said that to myself. I had to decide that or to leave her, to get a doctor. And then the rain began too. I needed a doctor. If the woman had only sent one . . ."

"You didn't recognise her? See her face?"

"Her back was towards me. She ran towards those houses, simply a woman in white, growing smaller. She was tall I think," her gaze swivelled, "and fair-haired."

"As I am?"

"Yes. At first I thought she had been frightened by some man, or was angry, had quarrelled perhaps. I waited."

"For how long?"

"I simply do not know. I cannot bear to think of that. To know that I sat there, and that if I had only hurried! But finally I called Bruno, fetched a stick, and my coat. When no one followed the woman I thought it could have been a snake she had seen."

Her words grew more rapid, telling of Bruno seeing the girl, of the pair of them diving into the creek and pulling her out, of the long minutes working over the girl and praying for help to come.

She looked exhausted when she had finished. "That is the whole of it." Her voice was harsh.

To give her time to recover composure Gabriel said idly, "You knew Carol Zamia, didn't you?"

"Yes." Again the little grimace marred her face.

"I believe," Gabriel went on, hardly realising what she was saying, her thoughts still filled with the running woman, "that she had—her mother called it a crush—on you and that . . ."

The elder woman moved impatiently. She went over to the table, opened a small wooden box, asked, "A cigarette, Mrs. Endicott? No? You do not mind if I . . ." a little gesture of taking one from the box finished the question. "I understand what you mean, but it was not that. It was . . . but you know the family perhaps? No? Then you must understand that Carol was . . . morbid, introverted, drawn back on herself. I do not know exactly how to explain." She was frowning. "But once she knew I was German, and a Jew, and saw this scar," she flicked back the cuff of her tangerine cardigan, "and knew that once there was a number tattooed there . . ."

"A concentration camp!" Gabriel blurted out the words, then stammered, "I'm sorry. You won't want to remember."

"Ah, you think the same as Carol?" The question was almost mocking. "But I was one of the lucky ones. I was not even found till six months before the war ended. I was in good hiding, you understand. Then I was sent away, but by then chaos was beginning. Another two months and we were moved and things were so confused thirty, forty, perhaps more of us, just slipped away and were never caught. It was so simple, by then. And I saw no real horrors, experienced none, except in my mind. In the imagination. But Carol," she shook her head, "she refused to believe it. 'Mrs. Buchanan,'" her tone was suddenly a child's, excited, expectant, "'do tell me . . .' It was useless to say, 'But I saw no terrible ovens. I saw few deaths and those only from natural causes; from disease and age; I saw no torture. You are a silly little girl, Carol. You are morbid. There are better things to dwell on than death and pain'.

"It was the same with this poor Bernice Strang. That subject was another fascination. In the end I grew very angry. 'Go away,' I said to her, 'And don't come back, Carol, till you have stopped dwelling on these bad things.'"

"Bernice Strang?" Gabriel had turned back to the telescope; was looking again at the creek. "Oh lord, yes, I remember now. She was knifed, wasn't she? And left in the river. It was just after Christmas of last year, wasn't it? I'd gone from Larapinta by then. My parents were dead and our home sold up for development and I moved away, but I read about it in the papers and Phil . . . my cousin . . . said it was a completely senseless crime. They never did find any motive, did they?"

"If so, it was never admitted. I remember when I bought this house a year ago—from your husband, Mrs. Endicott, did you know that? When I came here people spoke of it still. The work of a maniac they called it. I was warned not to walk alone in the scrub, in lonely places."

"Why was Carol so interested?" Gabriel swung away from the telescope.

Again the little marring frown crossed the woman's face. "A

pleasurable terror in dwelling on such a horrible thing?" she suggested. "And then, Carol worked in the toy store where Bernice worked before her. Baby-sat, also, where once Bernice did. That seemed to excite her. She dwelt on the prospect, continually, that one of these people she met and worked for had done away with Bernice. Once she had some terrible theory that a man had tried to . . . let us be delicate, unlike Carol . . ." her mouth twisted in faint disgust, "and say he tried to go too far with the dead girl and when she threatened to make trouble he knifed her in panic. Yes, that was Carol's great idea. I laughed. Carol was very angry." She clenched her small hands, stamped her foot, glared in a mockery of childish temper, 'But one man, Mrs. Buchanan, was bad to me, too.'" She relaxed, shaking her head, "She was a very silly child. A lonely one, too. Her home life . . ."

Gabriel broke in sharply, "Didn't you believe that some man had tried pestering her? What happened, anyway, or was supposed to have happened?"

"He drove her home from baby-sitting and pulled up in some lonely spot. She grabbed the ignition key and ran away. All the way home. That was her story. No, it was not true, Mrs. Endicott. She said it only because I laughed at her idea. She could never stand being an object of fun. To give her a little fright I said I would ring a policeman and say, 'Policeman, arrest this man', and I asked his name." She gave a little chuckle. "She knew then she had gone too far. She said he had apologised; she had promised not to tell; she must keep her word. Oh yes, she was a silly little girl, but there . . . she is dead. Yes, she's dead."

Gabriel shivered. She asked urgently, "Mrs. Buchanan, did you see this woman on the path? Before she ran away?"

"No. I went to the telescope only a tiny moment before she came running from the trees by the bridge."

"And she wore a white dress? A short white tennis dress?" she asked in sudden hope.

"No. Why are you so interested in this woman?"

Confused, dismayed, Gabriel swung round to face her, seeing a new alertness, a strangeness, in the dark eyes.

Was Lisa Buchanan, she wondered in panic, seeing in a new

37

light her visitor's youth, her fair hair and her compelling interest in the unknown woman?

She blurted out, "I was just wondering—I mean, it *was* an accident, wasn't it? This woman isn't supposed to have had something . . ." her voice trailed off under the shrinking distaste, the air of dislike, in the elder woman's face. Gabriel could almost guess her thoughts.

Another like Carol, the woman could have been reflecting; morbid, intent on discovering horror.

But there was relief in meeting the expression, because it meant that Lisa Buchanan's thoughts had turned away from the possibility that Gabriel herself had been the running woman of Monday evening.

. . .

"We'll expect you back then, when you've seen Mrs. B."

That had been Eileen Zamia's half-smiling, half-mocking farewell, together with the addition, "You don't have to help us, Gabriel. You know that. You needn't come back at all. But I hope you will, once you've seen Mrs. B and asked her all about it.

"It's not nice being called liars the way you've called us."

But, driving away from Lisa Buchanan's, Gabriel knew she wouldn't face the Zamias again and see the malicious satisfaction in Eileen's face. She was simply going to write out a cheque, place it into an envelope and put it into the letter-box by the gate. Home again, she would ring them, give a curt statement that the cheque was in the box and would be repeated each month till the running woman was found, and then ring off.

Out of sight of the house on the ridge she stopped the car, took her cheque book from her purse and scribbled the cheque. The envelope in which she placed it was one addressed to herself, sent unsealed with an account. She crossed out her own name, wrote in Eileen Zamia's and sealed the envelope before driving on.

When she turned into Pitt Road the scene was so startlingly different she instinctively slammed on the brakes. The silence and emptiness had been swept away in a swarm of children. Only

38

swarm described it. They crowded the footpaths with their games, overflowing on to the road with an apparent contempt for the possibility of traffic. Watching the scene, she thought that probably familiarity with the area had indeed bred contempt because local people would know the danger of turning a car into the road after school was out.

She left the car where it was; began to walk towards the Zamia house, and only then realised the complete absence of adults from the scene, the emptiness of the front gardens. It was as though the adult world of the housing estate had thrust the children outside the front gates and left them to their own devices.

In return they seemed to turn an unseeing gaze on adults, because it was as though she was invisible as she edged round their games. Even when she suddenly stopped, close to the Zamia house, and spoke aloud, she still stood ignored.

She said again, "You're Mark Zamia, aren't you?" staring down at the short sturdy figure in faded jeans and blue sweater who leaned against the green-painted wood fence, apparently lost in the blast of sound from the transistor radio held to his left ear. He was so like the photo of Carol, with the same coarse-springing hair as Fred Zamia, that she knew she was right.

But he went on ignoring her, and the two small girls who fought verbally, shrill attack and counter-attack, over a doll's pram, close to his feet.

Angry, suddenly sure that he knew she was there, she reached out a hand. His head jerked, the dark eyes changing so swiftly from blankness to recognition, that she realised she'd misjudged him; that he'd been completely lost to the world beyond the radio.

He said, "What y'want?" sidling away.

"Just to speak to you a moment." She had to raise her voice to be heard over the startling volume of sound round them, but nobody paid them the slightest attention. Smiling, hoping to win his good humour, she said, "That's a very nice radio."

"It was Carrie's . . ." he jerked, then was silent.

"Carrie? You mean . . . Carol?"

"Uh-huh. What y'want?"

"You know who I am, don't you, Mark?"

39

He nodded. He was still holding the transistor close to his ear, and a glaze of blankness was spreading over his dark eyes again.

Irritated, determined to hold his attention, to question him, she reached out her hand again. "Give me that for a moment." His resistance was so slight it was easy to ignore it. Her hand snapped off the sound, but then she went on gazing at the little radio. In surprise, and shock.

It wasn't a childish possession, she realised. There was nothing cheap about the case or the workmanship, or the brand name. The thing, small as it was, must have cost at least sixty dollars.

Still staring at it, disbelief gave way to blazing anger. Twenty-four dollars a month, regular, the thoughts mocked. A lie! It had to be that. The radio wasn't something Carol would have received as a present. She had been only a schoolgirl, with a Saturday job. How much had she earned from that? A dollar and a half? Two dollars? Saturday work would mean only three hours . . . then impatiently she brushed the question aside. However much work Carol had done baby-sitting, the sum total of her week's jobs couldn't have amounted to more than twenty-four dollars in a month, surely, and was it reasonable to suppose the girl would have handed it all over, without keeping a penny piece for herself?

It might have been, but for the radio. Even if the Zamias had guaranteed a hire-purchase deal on it, Carol would have had to pay a weekly sum—probably four dollars—because the radio was something that could be easily damaged, broken beyond repair. Almost certainly a hire-purchase agreement would entail it being paid off very quickly. And four dollars a week on the radio meant what? That Carol hadn't done much helping with family finances.

Gabriel asked, "This was Carol's? She bought it?"

"Uh-huh."

"I would have thought a girl your sister's age would have bought clothes rather than this. And make-up. Jewellery . . . things like that."

His shoulders lifted, so that his thick short neck, so like Fred Zamia's, became almost non-existant and his head was hunched, gnome-like, to his body.

"She'd gobs a'make-up." He moved uneasily, jerked out, "What's it to you?"

"Nothing, actually." She was sure that nothing in her voice or expression gave away her anger. Her hands tightened on the radio to prevent herself pulling out the cheque and envelope, tearing them into pieces. While the gesture would have relieved her pent-up anger, she knew it wouldn't get her anywhere. It would be far better to hand the cheque over for the moment, then get proof positive that Carol had never helped her family financially. It surely shouldn't be hard to find out how much she earned and spent on herself. There was pleasure, a relief from the afternoon's fear and humiliations, in dwelling on the prospect of facing the Zamias with proof of their lies, with denial of their right to what Eileen Zamia had called compensation.

Abruptly she handed the radio back, fumbling in her purse. She said crisply, "I want you to give your mother this, Mark. It's important. Do you understand?"

He took it without comment, his burdened hand immediately beginning to fiddle with the radio. She said sharply, "I want you to go straight inside . . ."

His thoughts, she was sure, were already turning away from her. He said, "Mum said to get t'hell outside till teatime."

"Then see she gets it then," she said helplessly.

He was already lost in glazed-eyed listening as she turned away. She was wondering, as she drove towards the shopping centre, if Eileen Zamia had said much the same thing to Carol that Monday evening. The boy had seemed to find nothing unusual in the order to get away from the house. Perhaps, she thought in sudden pity, Carol's urge for work had been not so much an urge for money, as an attempt to find somewhere to go.

And the toy shop seemed a pleasant enough refuge when she reached it. It was sandwiched between a supermarket and a children's wear shop, the two big windows filled with dolls and guns, tricycles and teasets. In one window a train pounded round and round a small circle of track; in the other a battery-driven bear drank every few seconds from an upraised cup, under the pop-eyed stare of a huge golliwog.

41

When she entered a ginger-haired man was talking to a woman with two small children clutching her print skirts. He looked up alertly, his gaze sliding over Gabriel appraisingly. She thought in wry amusement, watching him come towards her, that he evidently considered her blue suit and crocodile shoes and purse carried hope of more profit than his other customer.

But the smile on his young freckled face was pleasant. It remained so in the face of her blunt, "I'm not a customer, I'm afraid. Please attend to her," she nodded to the other woman, "I've time to wait."

"She's only looking." His tone was wryly resigned. "You're not in the trade?" His second appraising glance dismissed the idea, "So what?"

"I'm Mrs. Endicott. You may have known my husband, Nicholas."

Surprise lit his blue eyes. "*You've* come about the cistern?" then at her blank look he laughed openly. "No, I can see not. But Endicott's are the owner's agent for this place," he waved a hand round, "and I've done a moan, 'Landlord, landlord, me Loo leaks'!" At Gabriel's sudden chuckle, he said lightly, "Come into the office if you like."

The space so dubbed was hardly more than a cupboard. He gave her the unpainted wood chair, perched himself on a box, said, "I can't offer a cig. Sorry, but this place is inflammable . . ."

"I don't smoke anyway, Mr. . . ."

"Brown. Plain Brown."

At another time she might have fallen in with the mockery in his tone and voice and given back, "Well, Mr. Plain-Brown," but her mind was too tense, too concentrated on what she was going to say.

She began crisply, "Mr. Brown, I've come about Carol Zamia." She saw surprise come into his blue eyes again, and went on swiftly. "You probably know I'm carrying on my husband's work for the pool," while her mind mocked her words with the thought what a glorious chance Nicholas's work was for herself to talk about the dead girl. "Carol drowned. I'd like to know if she ever

42

mentioned swimming to you—ever expressed a wish to learn—ever spoke of how having no pool here . . ."

"Oh lor," he was shaking his head, the light catching the gold in the ginger of his curly hair, "you're right off the beam. I see what you're getting at, but look—I even had to tell her to wash. Blink away," he sounded defiant, "but it's true. She wore sandals here. Her toenails were filthy. And her hair was disgusting. She used to think a good dollop of nail polish, toes and fingers, a solid lather of face goo, and half a tin of hair spray, put on Friday nights I should guess, did instead of soap and water."

Gabriel's mouth compressed. She suggested, "She spent her wages on cosmetics?"

"No. I guess not. In fact, no definitely. The poor kid couldn't hold on to her two dollars—that's what I paid—for more than five minutes." He shrugged. "Her dad used to wait outside at midday, when we shut up, his hand ready waiting. Then off he'd nick with it to put on the gee-gees. That's why I wasn't hesitating in looking round for someone else. If I'd known she was getting something out of the job I'd have tried to stick with her. As it was . . . she was hardly going to lose anything, was she now?"

"You were letting her go." Gabriel spoke vaguely. She was thinking grimly that not even Eileen Zamia could claim that two dollars a week spent on horses was a necessity, yet she had spoken of them not being able to manage without Carol's help.

She became conscious he was waiting for her to say something. She jerked into speech, asked again, "You were letting her go . . . because you couldn't stand her?"

"That's it, or rather, not her, but her talk. Don't take any notice of me saying she didn't wash." He sounded half-ashamed now. "She was a good little tyke in some ways. Willing. She didn't mind dirty jobs, clearing up and all that. A lot of them kick if you so much as mention a broom. Carol didn't. I'd have smartened her up if I'd meant to keep her on, but I thought this place was bad for her. That sound funny? True, though. She'd gotten to think-ing about Berry so much it was like a disease. Bernice Strange, I'm talking about. You know?" At Gabriel's nod he rattled on, "It was like a bloke caught on the booze slide. The more she

43

thought about Berry being here, touching things, moving round here, the more she harped, yap yap yap, and the more about Berry she wanted to know . . . well, she was starting to get excited-drunk on it if you ask me. Starting to make up all sorts of wild theories . . ."

"I've heard one. Did she tell you some man had pestered her driving her home from a baby-sitting job? That she thought the same thing had happened to Bernice Strang, and the girl had meant to make trouble?" she asked idly.

His face went suddenly blank. He said shortly, "That's a new one on me. Anyway it won't wash so far's Berry's concerned. She was a decent kid, but she could slap a man down without any harm done. You get plenty of Peter-Pans in this business, the sort that never grow out of games and trick cigars, fake spiders and all the rest of that caper, and they act skittish to go with it. You know the sort of thing—a pinch when the shop girl's bending, slaps and tickles and a lot of double talk, and Berry was damn attractive." He gave a quick grin. "Nothing to me though. I'm content with the little blonde I said 'Have my worldly goods' to, two years back. Berry could handle it all without blinking—seemed to sum them up and treat each one to a different trick—had them squirming one minute and laughing with her the next. Came of growing up in Africa, I'd say—you know she came from there? She was hot as mustard on going back. I think there was some chap over there. She loved the place anyway, and out there she'd been used to handling natives, white men, the lot. Nothing tough about her, mind you, but a bloke that'd been to a party and got a bit tiddly, say, before he drove her home, wouldn't face her. She'd have handled it. It was a loony did for her. Seven goes with the knife he gave her. If that isn't loony, what is?

"But Carol had her own ideas—a different one every Saturday. I was a sort of sounding-board for her trying 'em out. Lord, some of them'd've made my old cat laugh. I lashed out with a verbal slap or two, but it didn't help so I said to myself, Out she goes, Les. This is bad for her. She needs a job where Berry never put a toe. So I was looking around . . . but lor, I've been gassing along like a politician. You should have slapped me down." He

44

gave a sudden rueful grin. "Berry would have handed me out a gobstopper. I never caught on at first why she carried round bags of sticky candy—big chunks of it—till it dawned on me sure as I started running on ear-bashing her to blazes, out came the packet and she was saying sweetly, 'Do have a candy, Les', and there I was, choked quiet for a good fifteen minutes.

"Now where were we . . . you asked me, didn't you now, if Carol wanted a swimming-pool and I said . . . lor, don't I babble, don't I just!

"You take it from me she wasn't interested. You're thinking maybe if she did there's a point for the district having a pool— kid died because she had nowhere to learn to swim, kind of set-up? Won't wash. I'm sorry, but you've got to face it. Carol liked comics, dogs, cream horns . . ."

"And cosmetics?" she said lightly, standing up. Apparently casually she said, "If her father took her wages from here I suppose that's why she went baby-sitting—to earn pocket money for herself."

He pulled a face. "Between you and me and that smirking Talkie-doll over there, I've had it from several sources he hung round those jobs too—public version, he was a good dad waiting to escort his darling home; private—your guess's good as mine."

He went with her to the shop door. The woman in the print dress was still absorbed in the small toys on the counter. He pulled a little face at her print-clad back, "A riot of business, isn't it? Trade's slack, that's the truth. Different Saturdays. That's why I had Carol." He looked suddenly anxious, "Don't you take notice of me babbling away, Mrs. Endicott, about her . . . I mean, she was a good little tyke really. And after all, she's dead . . ."

Never speak ill of the dead, she thought wryly. But Eileen and Fred Zamia weren't dead, and there were plenty of ill things to think and say about them. She sat in the parked car for several minutes, just thinking. The radio had suddenly become a nagging puzzle. If Carol had kept all her earnings she could have bought it, but seemingly she had been left with little, what with Fred waiting whenever he could to pounce with outstretched hand. And if he was that type he would never have guaranteed a hire-purchase

45

agreement for the girl—any money around he would have demanded for himself.

Which meant that Carol had either bought the radio for cash or been given it. The first idea wasn't feasible in the light of Fred's behaviour, and Carol's spendings on other things, but who on earth, she wondered, would give a child like Carol a sixty-dollar radio? It wasn't a secondhand one, she knew. It was shiny new and bright, a recent acquisition. Probably, she reflected cynically, before long Fred would sell it and put the proceeds on the horses.

But however she had gained it the fact remained that Carol definitely had not helped the family with their rent and bread and butter. There was satisfaction in that knowledge, an excited gloating in lifting the phone when she reached home and dialled the Zamia number.

She didn't bother choosing her words. They flowed out effortlessly, in an anger that died in weary satisfaction when the other woman didn't try to break in.

Only when she was finally silent did Eileen say crisply, "Well, a'course, Gabriel, I wouldn't deny that Fred took over Carol's earnings, but that's a dad's right and she was real soft, Carol was. Sometimes her brothers and sister'd get hold of her and whine about how about a doll or one of them matchbox cars, if you know what I mean, and Carol'd fall, she was that soft. I said to her over and over, 'Carol, that's no good. You've got to be hard sometimes, because what's more important, good milk and eggs or a matchbox car or truck?'"

"Presumably," Gabriel felt almost light-headed, "The children didn't wait for her in dark streets outside her baby-sitting jobs, in the hope of her buying them a matchbox truck on the spot."

"I never said how they did, now did I? Fred never did like Carol being out late and some of them men who've been having an evening out are half-seas gone when they get home. Not fit to drive a kid home after, Fred always said, 'nd then sometimes other kids'd hang round in groups waiting for her, knowing she'd have money hot in her hand, and say to her, if it wasn't too late, that the milk bar was open and what about it? Like I said, Carol was soft."

46

"But I'm not," Gabriel said flatly, definitely. "I'm told your husband simply wasted Carol's money on horses. That's not supporting your family."

"Well, a'course, Gabriel, there's folk'd say anything about anyone. Like what they're saying about Carol now. They're saying . . . it made me feel sick to the stomach, Gabriel. I had to get Fred run to the chemist's and get me a settling drug. They're saying all over the place now that maybe Carol was pushed in, deliberate.

"But a'course it's only talk. People plumping for reasons for her running off that way and never coming back. Still the police might start asking all sorts of questions . . . but a'course, Gabriel, you can count on me and Fred.

"But, y'know Gabriel, though I maybe shouldn't say it, Carol was always one for putting herself forward and being nosey. She was really interested in that photo of you I showed you and asked all sorts of questions about you. The kids know that. If the police started asking they might think Carol might've easy gone round and introduced herself to you. I did think maybe that could've happened. I gave out she was going to a teacher's place, only she really said nothing at all. Just took off. But with you being by the creek—well I said to Fred, maybe Carol was doing a little job for Gabriel, like maybe helping her start off a garden in that new place of hers. It's all bare earth, as I said to him, and there's some of the old Sturt land still not built on and still shrubs and that growing on it and what if Carol went over to help dig some up and was carrying a spade and such and that's how she came to trip and go over. Did it happen like that, Gabriel? With you maybe looking at the spade in your own hands and being frightened someone might say you'd hit her for some reason or other . . ."

Silently Gabriel replaced the receiver. She was shaking violently. After a while calmness came, but she was still sitting there, staring into blackness, when Phil came, so that when she finally dragged herself up and went to open the garden doors he exclaimed in relief, "My God, you frightened the life out of me! You were sitting there gazing at the glass with madwoman's eyes!"

All she could think of to say was an absurd, "I was planning what to have for dinner."

His expression went blank. He said mockingly, "Well all I can say is you must have been thinking of hemlock soup and meat balls with arsenic sauce, Angel," but the mockery didn't touch his dark, watchful eyes.

CHAPTER FIVE

"What've you been doing? Playing Madame Chairman to the Society for the Prevention of Tweaking Pussy-Cats' Tails?"

In spite of herself Gabriel smiled. It was impossible not to when Phil's clown-face was twisting in gentle mockery, but she asked dully, "Do you think it's fair to mock? You practically forced me into joining the pool committee. Remember your talk of vegetables? Of . . ."

He perched himself on top of the tangerine and white stool by the bench, stealing a curl of celery from the bowl of iced water.

"That was a start," he told her. "It's time for other things. When are you going to go downtown and sit behind Nick's desk and take over the job there?" he shot at her suddenly.

She nearly said, "When I've cleared myself of this horrible thing, when I've proved them wrong." Instead she blurted out, "I went to see the Zamias today."

His hand hovered over the iced water again, and was still. "So that's why you look so flattened. Why did you bother? Iley wouldn't have expected . . ."

"Iley?" she jerked. "Oh . . . you mean Eileen . . ."

"Didn't you call her that?" He was frowning. "But wait on—you never saw much of her, did you? How come . . . oh no, hold on!" He shook his head, mocking disapproval on his wide, clown mouth. "Don't tell me your darling mamma, as well as my own chuck-headed goose, coddled our Iley to death after that confounded party? And that you've been Kindly Remembered ever since, with those ghastly Christmas toffees . . ."

"Phil," she spoke without awareness of the sharpness in her voice, the strain in her expression, "was Eileen . . . Iley . . . badly hurt then? She didn't work after she hurt her arm, did she? She . . ."

49

"She married Our Fred, ducks," he said absently, but his gaze was puzzled. "Why so intense about it?"

"Oh . . ." she fought for some excuse, came up with a lamely-voiced, "I was remembering things today, realising I'd never asked at the time what happened to her after that accident. She mentioned how kind your mother was—she was telling me you'd sent flowers for Carol. Why didn't you tell me when I was talking about swimming and myself and a girl drowning, that it was her daughter?"

"I suppose I took it for granted you knew. Why?"

She brushed the question aside. "Anyway we got on to the subject of yourself and Aunt May and the old days."

"Mmmm? To be honest I don't think Iley was hurt as badly as the fuss warranted, but you know my dear goose . . ." his voice softened. "She adores coddling people. We were a most unsatisfactory brood of offspring, you know, Angel. Bursting with rude health and averse to coddling. You were better, but your mamma's province. Iley's arm, I suspect, was simply a heaven-sent chance to coddle unrestricted. Iley lapped it up, of course, but Our Fred stepped in and said enough was enough." He looked astonished, "which is a bit remarkable when I come to reflect on it as it seems he speaks about three words a year. Love must have spurred his tongue." He wrinkled his nose at her, laughing, "And lo, they lived 'appy ever after, ducks." Then he sobered, said flatly, "or rather, not so happily. I wouldn't put Iley down as a maternal-minded creature in spite of all those kids, but Carol's death was . . . filthy beastly, as we used to say." His dark eyes were suddenly bleak. "Gossip's having a field day—the latest idea being the poor kid was chucked off deliberately. Though for what reason gossip doesn't know. It's this woman of course . . . people are trying to drum up a reason for her bouncing off and never saying a word.

"You know, I've my own idea. I plump for the fact she couldn't swim."

She knew the shock, the fright, must show in her startled up-turned gaze, but he seemed oblivious of it.

"Well look at it—doesn't this seem reasonable? The two of

50

them aren't so far apart and suddenly the girl trips and falls. The woman rushes forwards. She can't swim and then to her horror she realises the girl can't either. Now what would *you* have done?"

"Run for help." The words seemed to stick in her throat.

"I'm damned sure you wouldn't have. You'd look round you— see how far all the houses were and try to help. You'd grab something like a tree branch, thrust it at her, try to let her grab it, or even try and thrust her with it, towards the bridge, so she could grab on to that. Now wouldn't you?"

"Yes," she admitted.

"And you'd scream for help, knowing that if anyone was near to you they'd come. But nothing happened. You were still alone and you couldn't reach the girl and she kept going under. I think you'd stay, Gabriel. You'd stay in the hope she'd come up and be able to struggle closer to you. You'd stay till the very end, till she went under and didn't come up. I don't think you'd try to wrench yourself away. You'd know there was no one close to you, or your screams would have brought them, and at any second she might just be close enough . . . well? Isn't it reasonable?"

"Yes."

"And then . . . you must have believed her gone for good. You'd run away, sick with shock. You wouldn't be able to bear the idea of having to tell the world about it; of the idea of having to face the girl's parents . . ."

It was so horribly plausible, so exactly what the whole world would say if the story came out of her, a non-swimmer, being by the creek, that it was unbearable.

She burst into rapid speech, saying the first thing that came to her tongue, "Did you ever give Carol a sixty-dollar transistor radio for a present, Phil?"

"Ouch!" His clown face dissolved into a lopsided leer. "Is that what you see now when you look at me? A nasty old man running after little girls? My dear Angel . . ."

Shocked surprise gave her no time to think. She blurted out, "Why didn't I think of that? If it was true . . . and she really did promise to keep quiet . . . it could be . . ."

"What are you babbling about?" He asked sharply.

"I . . . you mentioned gossip. Well listen to this piece. I heard a story today that Carol claimed some man had mauled her about. She refused to say who he was, only that he'd apologised handsomely and she'd promised not to tell. I just thought the radio could be the handsome apology. It's a beautiful little thing and she couldn't have bought it. I've heard . . ." she hesitated, said slowly, "I sound like a complete gossip-monger, don't I? But I heard that Fred took all Carol's money and put it on the horses."

He pulled a face. "Gambling's a drug so far as Fred's concerned. Iley takes over his whole pay and doles him out cash a dollar at a time to stop it all going down the drain. But he must have won sometimes. You can count on there being some arrangement that Carol took a share of that—he'd never have got the money out of her otherwise."

"Heavens, of course! I never thought of that. A good win could mean a radio. It was just that story and . . ."

He frowned. "You never got that story from Eileen Zamia. She'd have got the man's name out of the girl and created in a big way."

"It was from someone else. Actually it was connected up with Bernice Strang."

The bowl of water shook, half-toppled.

"Careful," she admonished. "Phil, did you know her?"

"Angel pet, I have what sometimes seems three thousand nephews and nieces. Remember? Bachelor uncles are regarded as good old money-bags. Of course I knew Berry. She worked in the toy shop."

"And she was killed. Knifed," she shivered.

"If it affects you like that why think about it?"

Surprised at the harshness of his voice she simply stared blankly.

She said in sharp annoyance, "Because someone mentioned her to me when we were talking of Carol and the girl being ghoulish, dwelling on horrors, being fascinated by working where the Strang girl had worked before her. Carol rather fancied herself as solving the crime. She thought Bernice had been mauled about coming home from some baby-sitting job, just as she had been herself. And the Strang girl had made a fuss, threatened to tell . . ."

"Just a sordid case of tiddly dad on the slap and tickle?" The harshness was still there in his face and voice, then his expression broke, lightened, creased into clown-like mockery, "and of course good old dad, respectable hub and father and all that, naturally carried a wicked sheath knife in his dinner jacket?"

She laughed, more from relief at his change of attitude than because she was really amused. She said, half-defiantly, "It needn't have happened that same night. He could have begged her to think it over. She did, but said she thought he should be punished . . ."

"Lumme!" He was suddenly the pop-eyed clown of their childhood. "Turn the page for a dramatic continuation . . ."

"Figs to you!" she retorted, equally childishly. "Seriously Phil, you must admit men who've played the fool have killed before now to stay put on their respectable little pedestals. Men do the maddest things when . . ."

"Women, too. Remember our running woman?"

She jerked. "Doesn't anyone have an idea who she is?"

"I doubt it. How many young, fair-haired women are there round this area? There's yourself for a start. Were you by the creek on Monday evening?" he mocked.

"No, no I wasn't."

As soon as the lie was out she was terrified for fear someone had seen her leave the bus in Larapinta and would tell, and he'd find she'd lied. She wanted nothing except to turn his thoughts from her youth, her fairness, her connection with the creek, her inability to swim. "Look, I've just thought—why couldn't the woman have seen someone push Carol? That's it—she saw Carol pushed and she's utterly terrified. She mightn't have . . . well perhaps she didn't see this person clearly, but she might think the person imagines she did. And the person . . . it could be the man who pestered Carol, couldn't it? And Bernice, too. Carol hit on the truth, you see, and he knew she'd never really keep quiet and the business of Bernice might be raked up and he'd . . ."

Her soaring aimless babbling had startled even herself. She

53

stared blankly at the prepared salad on the table. "Really Phil, that's . . ."

Her words were lost under his own, and then lost altogether in laughter as he emoted dramatically, "Ah, mon ami! Ze magnificent little grey cells!"

She was still laughing when he said quietly, "Gabriel, I want you to promise me not to talk about Carol . . . or this woman . . . anything to do with it."

"What?" The laughter was gone under surprise.

He said impatiently, "Don't talk, speculate, gossip, probe . . . whatever you choose to call it. This woman'll have to come forward. Or be dragged forward. Can't you see that every woman who has a finger pointed at her will hurriedly point elsewhere? Sooner or later the finger will move in the right direction and then . . . what will it be like then? Already half the district is totally convinced Carol was deliberately shoved off the bridge." As he saw her expression he nodded. "You didn't know, did you? And now you do it's no longer funny, is it?

"If she'd come forward in the first place she could have said anything and possibly been believed. Now . . . the longer it is before she's found the worse the rumours will get. Don't be a party to helping them along. Or one day, Angel," in spite of the mockery she knew there was no laughter in his mind, "you won't be able to look in the mirror and face yourself and like what you see.

"I'll tell you a little story." He wasn't looking at her. "Maybe it could be called Scandal in the Supermarket and some bright soul could make it into a slapstick yarn. Only it's not funny.

"The main character is that Collis woman who's a viper-tongued vixen at the best of times. Picture her lurking among the asparagus tins and the wheaty-bix, Angel," the mockery didn't touch his tired expression. "Picture her pouncing on another woman and suggesting that as this Miss Traill was at a tennis party on Monday evening she took a short-cut home across the bridge, handed Carol a short sharp smack for some unknown reason and in her white tennis dress went flitting away through the sunset— not, of course, realising the unfortunate brat was drowning."

He looked up, but she wasn't thinking of the enormity of

54

the scene, of the fear the woman must have felt. She was simply thinking, Miss Traill—I have to see her.

Then he said, "And she has grey hair, Gabriel."

"Grey?" she jerked in astonishment, "But . . ."

"Grey might be mistaken at a distance for fair hair. Think of it, Gabriel—every woman with grey hair, white hair, fair hair . . . pointed out, whispered about . . ." he slipped his arm round her, said with concern. "Hold on, Angel. Stop shaking. It's not that bad. It can't hurt you. You weren't there. You can say where you really were; laugh at pointing fingers . . ."

For a moment there was only wild temptation to tell him the lot; to throw everything at him and let him solve it all as he'd solved so many of her childhood problems. Instead she blurted out, hopefully, "Miss Traill . . . *is* she . . ."

He let his arm fall away from her. "If her story's true, she's not. She had her bicycle with her. Oh yes, I was there. I took her home. Grabbed my beans and bread under one arm and Miss Traill under the other and dragged her out of the crowd. But no, I can't laugh about it," he sounded suddenly terribly tired. "It wasn't so much the Collis creature, or the other woman's shocked face, or the actual words or . . . it was those eyes. And gaping mouths. A circle of gaping mouths sucking it all in greedily. Fanciful? Perhaps. But horrible.

"She told me about it on the way home. She went to a tennis party at her sister's, true enough. But she wasn't on foot. And she never saw another soul. She never *looked*. She kept saying that, and wringing her hands. All she was thinking about was getting home ahead of the storm. She was looking at the sky—she told me it was like a big cauldron of black cloud with red fire coming out of it."

Gabriel said, "I know," and stopped, aghast. She said throatily, fighting panic, "I was looking at it, too. I thought it was going to pour. I remember reciting that old bit about red sky at night, washerwoman's delight and thinking it wouldn't be true, because the sky was angry and the light was so odd."

"That's right. She said it was the light made her think of the yellow dress."

"*Yellow* dress?"

She was unconscious of her hands clasping in white-knuckled anxiety on the edge of the table. Her thoughts clamoured. Someone in a yellow dress by the creek.

She asked the question urgently, frantically almost, then, seeing the swift surprise go leaping into his dark eyes, she forced herself to relax, to grimace, to say in pretended disgust, "I'm as bad as the rest! I'm just . . . one of those gaping mouths. Aren't I, Phil? Avid for . . ." She broke off, then said evenly, "There was someone in a yellow dress she saw by the creek?"

"No. I told you she didn't see anyone there. She was thinking of Mrs. Brown. Wife of the toy shop owner, you know. Well, don't stare," he shook his head at her, "Didn't I tell you that every woman who was named or pointed out would point somewhere else? There's nothing in it. Just a desperate attempt to get the heat off herself. It's abominable, yet understandable of course. But now you know—you can see for yourself what it's like . . . out there," he gestured towards the windows, "out in the big wide world you've been shunning for so long. Perhaps it's as well you're still shunning it now," he touched her cheek suddenly and smiled at her. "It's a thoroughly unpleasant corner of the world at the moment. Go on shunning it for now. And don't add your gossip to the rest."

She pressed, "Why should she think of this Mrs. Brown? And a yellow dress? If she didn't see . . ."

"I told you. It was nothing. Just a finger pointing away from herself. Leave it."

"Leave it!" she began, her head jerking up. Her lips parted again, then closed. She knew she wasn't going to tell him, see suspicion in his eyes, hear his questions. She couldn't have borne it. She could have dealt with the questions, even the suspicion, if only the nagging fear wasn't there in her mind that instead of dying away, the suspicion would flare into certainty and that along with the Zamias he'd finish by asking, "Why did you run away, Gabriel?" by saying, conviction in his voice, "You were the running woman. Weren't you?"

CHAPTER SIX

Miss Traill's home was what one of Nicholas Endicott's sales sheets might have described as "a little gem for the handyman". The iron gate sagged lightly, the front edge dragging, further scarring the cracked concrete drive, as Gabriel thrust it open. There were patches of rust showing through the blistered green paint; more rust on the front door bell as though the little wooden house with its dingy white paint held few visitors.

There was a light shining from a side window when Gabriel went up the path, but no one answered her ringing. She went on turning at the bell screw grimly, feeling rust on her fingers. Finally she simply stood there wiping the stain away in slow, deliberate strokes, while she fought down the rising anger that urged her to batter at the door, to demand that the woman inside open up, because she was sure that someone was there. Certain of it, when she moved round the side and saw the lighted window was now dark.

Anger was suddenly gone then, leaving only a shrinking pity, a quivering fellow-feeling for the woman inside, afraid to open her door, to face the world's eyes. She wondered if there in the dark the woman was standing with panic-stricken face, wondering if someone else like Mrs. Collis was waiting outside.

She went to the darkened square of window. She pressed her face to the slight gap at the bottom of it between the frame and glass. She said loudly, clearly, "Miss Traill, it's Gabriel Endicott, Phil Sturt's cousin. He told me he'd brought you home. I came to see if you were all right. Are you?"

The light came on, blinding her, making her eyes water. Then they cleared. She saw the pale face looking at her from inside the room. The woman said breathlessly, "You must excuse me. I was . . ."

"Frightened?"

Equally simply the woman returned, "Yes." Then she asked, "would you come round to the back door? I've been painting the hall."

A moment later Gabriel was being ushered through a kitchen where an ancient cooker huddled against a cracked sink, and into the smartness of new paint, new furniture, in the tiny living-room. Her hostess went on brightly, as though the incident of the darkened room and the unanswered bell had never happened, "A detestable job. Painting, I mean, of course. Or rather, not the painting itself, but the washing down first . . ."

She went on talking, smiling, not letting her visitor speak. Then abruptly the smile was gone, with the affability and ease of manner. Her body, in the long grey dressing-gown, seemed to sag. Lines showed clearly in her pale skin under the greying hair. She said wearily, "It was very nice of you to come." Her thin, veined hands were playing with the grey satin belt of the gown. "He . . . Mr. Sturt . . . told you, of course, what happened?"

"Yes. He said," Gabriel's intent gaze was searching for a sudden flood of colour in the pale cheeks, for a clenching of the veined hands, for anything that might hint the words were a lie, "that it was nonsense you being accused like that, because for one thing you weren't on foot. For another . . ."

The woman said rapidly, "That's so," and the words and her expression held conviction so complete hope slid away. She went on, "I took my bicycle with me. Of course I did. And later on I was thankful for it because of the storm coming. I only got off the cycle to cross the bridge. I remember almost running across and mounting again and hurrying on. The sky was so . . . well, vicious isn't the word, but . . . and the light . . ."

Gabriel said sharply, "Yes, Phil mentioned it, and a yellow dress. And Mrs. Brown."

The veined hands were still, holding tightly to the grey satin belt. She didn't say anything, and in desperation Gabriel asked, "why did you think the woman could be Mrs. Brown? You must have some reason. You . . ."

"I shouldn't have said it. Anything." The hands were moving again, twisting and pleating. "It was . . . the instinct to strike back

—show that someone else beside myself could have been there, could be . . . and now you're going to go on wondering. So will Mr. Sturt. And there'll be other people who'll suggest her. She's fair. She's young. And . . . well, on Monday she wore this very pale lemon frock—a sort of overall really. I was there in the shop. She works there nowadays. She has done since the child was born, since Bernice Strang died. It's jealousy, of course, understandable during her pregnancy, when things were hard for her, but it's ridiculous now. There was some trouble then—she grew quite unattractive, bloated, poor thing, and there was Bernice, so pretty, so unencumbered, always at *his* side. Bernice, I know, was going to leave as soon as the baby was born, only of course she died . . ."

The breathless voice was suddenly quiet. "When the baby was born," she went on after a little, "they got Carol to help on Saturdays. Mrs. Brown helped on weekdays. And Carol . . . she heard all that talk about Bernice of course. She was old enough to know what jealousy was. I heard her one Saturday, you see. Carol was speaking of the other girl for some reason and said, 'You loathed her though, didn't you, Mrs. Brown?' and her face was adult . . . knowing. Mrs. Brown didn't speak. She saw me and turned away, but her expression told a lot.

"Then, last Monday . . . I was in the shop and Mrs. Brown was packing toys. She told me she had to deliver the two parcels, and she was angry . . . no," she amended quickly, "not that. Cross, put out, anxious about it rather. Their van had broken down, you see. I could see the address on the box she'd already packed. It wasn't far from my sister's home, across the bridge, and I offered to take them myself when I went over to tennis, but she pointed out I'd find them difficult to manage on a bicycle.

"Then she added, 'I hope to get hold of Carol to carry one for me and I'll take the other'."

"But . . ."

The other woman said sharply, "I know what you're going to protest—that she's never said a word about it. Maybe she doesn't dare. Oh yes, perhaps she never asked the girl at all, but . . . what if she did? What if she daren't mention the toys now because there on the bridge Carol spoke to her the same way she did that Saturday only a fortnight ago? Then . . . that day . . . I thought Mrs. Brown would hit her. What if she did, while they were coming back across the bridge? What if Carol was given a slap that spun her round, jerked her foot from her shoe?

"That," her pale face darkened with a dull flood of red, "is what that frightful creature in the store suggested. Oh, not about Mrs. Brown. But putting *me* there on the bridge. Hitting the child. Though why should *I* have? I had no quarrel with her. I barely knew her. But it *is* possible, isn't it, that she was hit, and . . . the person . . . ran away in shame, in fright, not knowing she couldn't swim. They'd run home, wouldn't they, and wait for a phone call? For Carol's parents to come to their doorstep. And then afterwards . . . she wouldn't be able to admit it." She drew a long breath, "If it was Mrs. Brown . . . but it needn't be . . . I'm only guessing. There's . . ."

The veined hands were abruptly still again, holding tightly to the grey satin. The thin body in the grey dressing-gown was taut and still, the face expressionless. Only the grey eyes seemed alive— their quick glance darting, questioning, arguing, answering, speculating as the woman appeared to look at her visitor closely for the first time.

Her voice came finally in a harsh demand, "Just who are you?"

There'd been no conscious thought in Gabriel's mind of hiding her hair when she slipped the patterned scarf over her head before leaving the house. No conscious thought, she told herself in fierce defiance of the open suspicion in the speculating grey eyes, because all the time the veined hands had pulled and tugged and pleated at the grey satin her own slim fingers had been untying the knot of the scarf, letting it fall back.

She said, quite evenly, "I've told you. I'm Gabriel Endicott, Phil Sturt's cousin." She asked, "Why should I have lied?"

"You might be anyone. I've never seen you before. Perhaps," the woman stood up, "You came here just to find out if I ever *had* seen you before?"

Why didn't I think of this? The question nagged at Gabriel as she slowly stood up. Why didn't I think if the running woman was there in the store, or heard about that scene, she'd want to know everything Miss Traill might have seen, might know, about that evening.

She said, still quite evenly, "I know what you're thinking and suggesting, but it's nonsense. I'm simply Phil's cousin, who came to see if you were all right." The lie came effortlessly from her lips this time, "I wasn't near the creek on Monday."

The elder woman said nothing, only began moving towards the door. Gabriel said to her thin, grey-clad back, "But I hadn't thought till now that the woman might come here, or ring you . . ."

The grey head jerked. The woman turned slowly. She said, "She'd be fairly sure, wouldn't she, that I know nothing about her or I'd have spoken out long ago. She wouldn't come prying. not unless . . . she had another excuse for seeing me. Would she?"

The watchful grey eyes asked silently, Are *you* the running woman? Why did you run? Did she fall? Or did you slap her? Push her?

CHAPTER SEVEN

Gabriel forced herself to ignore the mocking intimacy in the use of her Christian name; the mockery of the, "I was real worried, Gabriel. I said to Fred after, maybe I've got her worried sick, what with her putting down the phone that way last evening. I was going to ring again, but Fred said let it be, that soft-soaping never helped a sick conscience and you knew we wouldn't let it out."

She broke across the words without commenting on them, asking, "I just rang for one thing—to ask if Carol was doing a job for the Browns on Monday evening? Delivering some toys across the creek?"

"Why no, Gabriel. Not to say a'course that Lady Brown . . . you'll excuse me, Gabriel, but that's what our Carol called her the way she put on airs. Put them on with me when she rang Monday. Wanted Carol to go round after school. Demanding, like. I said Carol was a free agent. When I told her she said, 'Not likely, mum. Lady Brown'll sneak out on paying me with some excuse or other—say I'd busted something and I was squaring it up by working today.' Carol'd been caught that way a'fore. Oh no, Gabriel, she wasn't doing any job for *them*, but then a'course you know that right well, don't you?"

The shrilly aggressive voice went on and on. Gabriel held on to the receiver, but she wasn't listening. She was thinking, with a slow plummeting of hope, that it had to be true. If the Zamias had had the chance of claiming some compensation from the Browns they would have done so.

She was reflecting on that as the voice went on. She cut across it with a startled, "But of course!" Then, as swiftly, not thinking what she was saying, that she was breaking a promise, she went on, "but what if Carol met Mrs. Brown when they were both going to cross the bridge and Mrs. Brown asked her then, as

62

she was going over, or even . . . Mrs. Brown could have been coming back when they met . . ."

Her voice trailed into silence. She was appalled at what she had done; what suspicion she had put into the greedy little listening mind; at the breaking of her promise. Then she remembered that already someone must have spoken a suspicion aloud of Mrs. Brown. The girl had admitted it.

So the promise didn't matter, but the suspicions she might have roused in Eileen Zamia did.

Then the woman said, "Now that's not very nice, Gabriel, is it? You're making out that because Lady Brown and our Carol didn't get on that she might've given Carol a shove for not agreeing to help her over the bridge with the parcels?"

Just that, Gabriel reflected. If the woman had been burdened with the parcels and the girl had refused to help, a shove could have resulted, an angry thrusting, "Then get out of my way, you little wretch!"

Then she remembered that the running woman had carried no parcels. So it couldn't have happened that way. The toys must already have been delivered. They must have met, face to face, on the bridge, coming in different directions and then . . . an angry exclamation, perhaps, from Mrs. Brown, a sharp, "You were coming this way but you wouldn't help me, you mean little wretch!" and perhaps a rude retort from Carol, a slap . . . it was even more plausible, she thought hopefully, than Miss Traill's suggestion of the girl taunting Mrs. Brown about the past.

She realised that Eileen was still speaking, was saying, ". . . not nice at all and it won't help."

"What? What won't?"

"Why, you making up these stories. And it's not true. Even if Lady Brown had shoved our Carol, she can swim and she knew Carol couldn't."

But Miss Traill had suggested the woman mightn't have remembered, Gabriel reflected.

"And then Miss Traill—I heard that one," the shrill voice pressed remorselessly on. "I said to Fred last night, what if Gabriel is scared sick people might start wondering about her not swimming and being fair and all, and she's starting stories about other people. And Fred said, 'Well if it comes to other folks getting hurt we'll have to speak out fair and honest'."

"You mustn't!" It was out before she had time to think; before she could stop the words. Only when they were spoken did she realise she'd fallen into another trap; that her listener must surely be convinced she was right.

She began, "I didn't start those stories, I . . ."

"Well I should hope not I'm sure, Gabriel, but human nature's human nature and it's natural you'd be scared sick of folk coming to suspect these things of you and all. But unless we got to we won't speak out. Only thing is . . ."

The silence stretched, grew, became something that simply had to be broken, but she couldn't force her tongue into speech and Eileen Zamia seemed content to let the silence remain for ever.

Finally she said, "The funeral, Gabriel. We got a shock."

A shock, Gabriel thought wearily. A shock? Why?

The woman said, "When it happened we never thought of expenses and that. Well, a'course that was natural, we were that upset. But soon's the police had let us call in the undertaker we did. I remember at the time he was talking of headstones after and a pile a'that and as I said to Fred when we were alone again, what does the basket think we are—millionaires? But we never gave a real thought to expenses and now the bill's turned up. Don't wait long, do they? And well . . . we just can't pay it, Gabriel. I turned sick when I saw it and me being this way and all, well a'course I can't work and get the money and Fred said, maybe Gabriel'll see her way to giving us a loan. For six months or so see, till the kid comes and I stop feeding it and can go to work and start earning. And I said, well Gabriel is helping this way right now and Fred says . . . he says there wouldn't have been no need for a funeral maybe, but for you, Gabriel."

It was abominable.

Gabriel could feel the tremor of the receiver against her ear, feel the trembling through her whole body. She started to speak, but the voice was whining now, but still pressing remorselessly, "I don't know what's got into Fred. He's acting so strange. It's shaken him up badly. Didn't sleep last night. I know, because I didn't either . . ."

She thought, If I were that woman how would I react to this? It would be enough to drive any woman, tortured by conscience already, into a breakdown.

Perhaps that's what they want, she thought in shrinking disgust. They'll only be satisfied when I'm a quivering, shrinking travesty of womanhood.

The woman was saying, "It's not as though we got anything to sell for the funeral money, lord knows . . ."

Her voice shrilled, "What about that radio? It must have cost sixty dollars. At least! Where did you get it?"

"Why Gabriel, I thought you'd've known. Phil gave it to Carol. We wouldn't sell that. It was the last gift she ever had, poor little tyke."

"Phil? That's a lie . . ."

"Excuse me!" The woman sounded outraged. "That it's not. Phil gave it her. Only a few weeks back."

.   .   .

The landlord of the Larapinta Hotel was busily counting. Though the genial smile remained fixed on his wide mouth, and he was apparently listening to the conversations going on round the section of the bar where he stood, he was counting glasses, wondering if the two truck drivers who had recently drifted out the bar door were simply on the footpath finishing their drinks or whether they'd gone into the toilets and he'd later find the glasses there, or whether they'd gone back to their truck and taken his glasses with them.

"Blast 'em," he muttered, "always running off with m'glasses . . ."

"Glasses, you say?" Abruptly he became conscious the muttered words had been half-heard, that he was the centre of attention. "You say she had glasses?" the little earnest man in front of him was asking. "First I've heard of that—just fair, and a white dress I heard . . ."

The landlord frowned. "I wasn't talking about women running —I was talking about my glasses running off. Not her. You know what I think? She couldn't swim. That's all. Tried to get the kid out, couldn't, thought she was done for, rushed off to get help and passed out. Came round again, see, then saw this woman and the dog. Thought to herself 'Well, that lets me out. I can go home and no one'll know and I won't be involved'. So off she goes."

He nodded in conviction. "That's it, I'll bet you a dollar. D'you know one bloke came in a while back and started chivvying the other blokes about their wives—Can they swim, he wanted to know. So there's plenty of others think like I do. God help us, he even asked my wife!" he gave a sudden rumbling chuckle.

"Oh? And *can* she swim?"

"Bet?" He smiled broadly. "It's the best bit of flattery she's had in a couple of years. She can't swim, right enough, but, 'me young and fair and able to run?' she says, and she nearly died laughing. I tell you she was the same age as me when we married, though she claims we're twelve years apart now. And she's fifteen stone into the bargain. She's out there in the wash-house right now still laughing.

"Still, you know," his voice slowed. "There was one in white I saw m'self. Got off the bus opposite. Must have been sitting at the back—she got out the back door and maybe not anyone noticed her to speak of. I was outside sweeping up a mess of paper some kids had dropped from ice-sticks on the pavement and I saw her hurrying off. She was young and fair and in white." He grinned. "Nice figure, too. I've seen her somewhere, but I can't put a name to her yet." He frowned. "It'll come to me sometime. Where I've seen or met her."

CHAPTER EIGHT

A night's inaction had been forced on her. She had wondered, ringing time after time, if Lisa Buchanan was simply sitting there in her house on the ridge, refusing to answer. Gabriel had cried aloud to her own silent house, "Doesn't she realise how important it is? That she's the only one who can help at all," and then had mocked at herself with rueful impatience because of course the woman couldn't know. She must be sure she had told everything she could. She wouldn't be thinking that there was someone else who had to question and question, squeeze every tiny second of that evening out of her mind.

In the end she had driven to the ridge. Even when her ringing and knocking weren't answered, she'd sat for a long time in the car, hoping the woman would come home, or even that the lights would suddenly spring to life inside the house—that the woman was sitting there in darkness, as Miss Traill had done, waiting for her visitor to leave.

Even the nagging thought of Phil's deliberate lie, the careful plotting out to her of how Carol could have gained the radio, had had to stay with her all night, because his phone wasn't answered either; his door wasn't opened, and finally sheer weariness sent her home.

She almost fell into exhausted sleep while creaming away her make-up. She simply fell across the bed, scrabbling the covers over her tired body, and when she woke it was far too late to catch Phil before he went to the office. Almost too late to catch Lisa Buchanan, because when the woman opened the door she was dressed in a suit and wide-brimmed hat; was in the middle of pulling on white gloves.

But at Gabriel's dismayed, "You're going out," she shrugged.

"It isn't urgent. I am one of those maddening souls who are always ready for an appointment half an hour too early. So . . ."

a little tilt of her head, a slight backing of her small slim body, gave invitation to enter, "perhaps you will save my friend the exasperation of having me arrive when she is . . ." her hands sketched descriptively, "curlers, face pack, uncorseted bulges."

Her mouth laughed, but her dark eyes seemed wary, considering, reflective—might even have been Miss Traill's. Gabriel wondered if it was deliberate that the elder woman showed her into the telescope room, went to the instrument itself, tilting it a little, or whether it was a reminder of Monday, a reflection of a thought that dwelt on the possibility her visitor was the running woman.

Gabriel said simply, "I've come to ask if you can't possibly tell something more about this woman," and saw first stark astonishment and then cold speculation in the other face.

"Now why should you imagine I would keep anything back?" she demanded.

"I didn't suggest that. What I hoped was that you'd have remembered something more about her. You must have thought of it all so many times since Monday . . ."

"I want to stop thinking," was the blunt reply.

"But you mustn't. You can't!" Gabriel urged. "Haven't you heard what's happening? What people are saying? Didn't you hear one woman accused another . . . in the middle of a store . . . in front of witnesses . . . and she . . . she accused someone else in turn. And this other woman . . . who's *she* accusing now, do you think?" She looked at the woman, saw her small body shrinking away and said, "Oh no, it's not a figment of my imagination. It's happening. And it has to stop. The first woman—she can clear herself, I'm sure. For one thing she had her bicycle with her. She could have cycled for help and you'd have seen the bicycle, wouldn't you?"

"A bicycle?" Astonishment was back. "She was on foot, I tell you."

"I know. And she was wearing a tennis dress and you said the woman you saw wasn't. Another thing, she isn't fair, but her accuser suggested grey hair would look much the same at a distance . . ."

"No!" Lisa Buchanan was shaking her head definitely. "This woman was young. Fair-haired."

"Long fair hair? Loose—you'd have seen it moving as she ran, wouldn't you? Or cut quite short?"

There was a long silence before the answer came. "I don't know. I can see it clearly in memory, but . . . there is simply light shining on fair hair, a white dress—and no, not a short tennis dress. This . . . had sleeves?" She seemed to be questioning herself in little abstracted murmurs now. "Or else . . . yes, I am sure there were long sleeves. Definitely not a tennis dress."

Gabriel couldn't speak; could only remember the cream jersey suit, the long sleeves. She tried to form her tongue round words, but it refused to obey and then the woman suggested, "Perhaps a cardigan, do you think? Buttoned over a white dress, or skirt?"

Gabriel found her voice again, jerked out, "That could mean a tennis dress after all."

"No. I think not. I can see her legs moving. I'd say her skirts were on the long side. Definitely not abbreviated."

"Many older women wear long tennis skirts," Gabriel said sharply.

"Perhaps, but there again we come to her hair. I am quite sure it was fair. Not grey. Nor white like my own. I can see the light shining on it, but I can't remember noticing if it was long or short. In any case long hair could be worn in a French pleat, a chignon, at times."

Not a short skirt, Gabriel was reflecting, but not an older woman either. A young woman, in an everyday dress. Perhaps with a cardigan over it. Or a woman like Brown's wife, young, fair, in a pale yellow overall? But would, she wondered, a girl of that age have longer-than-usual skirts?

She questioned as to how Lisa Buchanan could be sure about it. A woman running would bend her knees. That could make skirts seem longer than they were actually. She put the question but the elder woman simply shrugged. She said, with a faint underlying irritation in her voice, "How can I answer that?"

"Then can you remember her shoes?" Gabriel pressed.

"Of course! There were no tennis socks. I am quite, quite certain. If there had been socks I might have thought first of a girl—someone Carol's age. And no, no tennis shoes either. Not even white shoes, I am sure. Darker ones. But not high heels either. A woman's run in high heels is a sort of . . . waddle?" she smiled faintly. "Perhaps walking shoes—bronze, tan, brown, perhaps."

Gabriel knew a pulse must be jerking in her throat, betraying her perhaps to those reflective eyes. She was thinking of the white jersey suit, the jacket revers bound in tiny brown and white checks that matched the bronze buttons and mid-heeled pale bronze shoes and bag.

"Was she carrying anything?" Abruptly she remembered the storm, remembered Phil saying the woman would have tried to reach Carol with whatever was handy. "What about an umbrella?"

"I never saw her hands. Only her back." She asked sharply, "You think if she had an umbrella it would be more natural for her to use it to try and poke the girl's body towards the bank, than simply to run . . . but then the girl might have been well away from the bridge—she was a little distance from it when I came, and a little distance too from the bank. The woman might not have been able to reach her with it . . ." she broke off, frowning, and then said sharply, "and if she had wanted to help she would have dived in. Unless she could not swim herself. Is that what you are suggesting? That she did not come along later? She came as Carol fell, or was struggling? And that she might have tried to reach the girl with an umbrella . . ."

"An umbrella could be a weapon, too." She babbled on, not really thinking of what she was saying, wanting to fill the silence with words, turn the woman's thoughts from thinking of a woman who couldn't swim. "Mightn't she have hit at the girl with it—giving her a good whack across the buttocks even, the way you'd do with a naughty child—if the girl had jeered at her, and been rude and unpleasant, when she was taxed with being there after she'd refused to help with the toys . . ."

"Toys? Helping with toys?" She made a little gesture of distaste, "Why look shocked *now*, when you have put the suggestion into my mind? You're suggesting Mrs. Brown, aren't you? Thinking of that old tale. I would say Mrs. Brown was the last person

70

to have hit the wretched child!" She sounded angry, impatient. "A woman—you know this yourself, surely—never easily forgets she has made a fool of herself, made an item of gossip of herself. She would go out of her way to avoid a repetition of that other loss of control over the Strang girl. She'd remember only too well the sniggering, the gossip . . ."

"I thought you didn't come here till after she was killed?" Gabriel said sharply.

"Mother of God!" The elder woman threw up her hands. "Now look at me as though I am a criminal. Why? Do you imagine I am so saintly that when people gossip to me I shut my ears to normal curiosity? When I came here people were avid to tell me of Bernice, to say Mrs. Brown would be glad; to regale me with the whole sorry tale of the poor creature's jealous scenes. Do you imagine," the dark eyes were bitter, "that all that would not have scarred the woman's mind? Do you imagine she didn't, when she was well again, realise what a fool she had been; vow never to give another chance for gossip about her. Oh no, Mrs. Endicott, she is the last person in the district likely to have struck the girl."

Gabriel was shaking, was unable to still her body, or the tongue that cried, "But the most likely, if she did hit out, to run away. Wouldn't someone . . . like us . . . try to retrieve the situation, pull her out, bribe her to silence with the warning that if she said anything we'd call her a liar and be more likely to be believed than herself? But Mrs. Brown? Carol disliked her for a start. She'd almost certainly speak out from sheer spite. And people would remember the past, wouldn't they? The bad temper, the silly behaviour . . . and they'd be more likely to believe Carol than Mrs. Brown. So wouldn't she be the most likely one to run, if . . ."

"So," the woman's features were ugly with contempt, "you suggest Mrs. Brown let her drown deliberately? Why look so shocked? If it was Mrs. Brown who hit her, she must have known the child couldn't swim; could never live to tell her story, for the fact of running would then make it much worse for her. I am far from a fool, Mrs. Endicott. When you came here you were frightened and alarmed. You are trying to draw facts from me about this woman. You seem to want to prove her to be Mrs. Brown. Why? Because someone has pointed a finger at you yourself? Can you swim, Mrs. Endicott?" she shot out with sudden violence. "Can you? Could you have met Carol on the bridge and slapped her? And run, because . . ."

"But that's ridiculous. I didn't even know Carol."

"No? I admit to human curiosity. I was curious enough about you to mention you to friends last night. You are a cousin of Phillip Sturt, the architect. And he and Bernice Strang were enemies. And Carol was a very silly little girl. Add together those three things and speculate . . ." her eyes were mocking. "Not impossible, is it, to imagine Carol meeting you—did you really not know her?—and deciding to tease you perhaps with a naughty story of how your cousin did away with the Strang girl, and then, smack, a fall . . . did you carry an umbrella? Try to get her out? And fail? And run away . . . can you swim, Mrs. Endicott?"

As before she lied, desperately, "Of course I can. I grew up here, near the creek. Of . . . of course I learned to swim," but all she could think about was the impossible fact that Phil had lied about his relationship with Bernice Strang. Lied, too, about the radio.

How many other lies had he told her? Even more important, why had he lied at all?

• • •

She drove away sure she had allayed suspicion for a while at least. She had told the elder woman simply that her name had been mentioned, among others, and she'd been horribly shocked. She had seen the tenseness go out of the small body and dark eyes opposite, but the elder woman had said bluntly, "I doubt if anyone will ever know who she was. She must have been certain she wasn't seen. Won't talk soon die away, in any case? Those who throw mud at you now will forget and . . . would you want them as friends? Do you lose anything by knowing they are ill-natured? And what would you have me do? Try to prove blame when all I saw was the back view of this woman?"

Then she asked brusquely, "Why don't you take a little holiday? The past months have been bad for you. That is why you've let a few unpleasant words prey on your mind. Go away. Right away. For a fortnight, a month, longer . . ."

"Soon . . . a fortnight at the most . . . I have to take over my husband's business. The manager Phil got for me won't stay longer."

She was suddenly sick with fright of the thought of sitting in Nicholas's chair, talking with people, meeting people—seeing speculation and accusation in eyes, while rumour and counter-rumour went circling round and round; till she was asked in the open—perhaps as Miss Traill had been asked—"were you by the creek on Monday? Did you hit Carol? Can you swim?"

Would there, on that day, be someone, like Lisa Buchanan, to suggest Carol had teased her, taunted her with some silly story there on the bridge?

What was she going to say if they did? Say, "But I would have laughed, because I didn't so much as know he knew Bernice Strang. And when I asked him he lied . . ."

She couldn't go away without asking him why, and suddenly she was realising that if she went people might say she was running away, that she *was* the running woman, hurrying away to avoid questions she couldn't answer.

She said, "I can't go away. I've too much to do," and remembered here was still another problem to be attended to. The Zamias. And their demand . . . because that was what it was . . . that she pay for the funeral.

But she wasn't, she decided grimly, going near them to ask for the bill. She was simply going to the undertaker's and say she wanted to pay for the expenses. Do it and send the Zamias the receipt. She was, she decided, going to meet all further attempts to mentally twist at her with a prompt acceptance of conditions, and no argument at all. It was the only way to cope with Eileen's hate, she was certain. The woman was getting some perverted satisfaction out of her victim's twistings and turnings. Take that pitiful satisfaction away and Eileen would sooner or later give up

73

her persecution. What would be the point of it? And why spare time for worrying, for fretting, for raging over the Zamias, when all her thoughts ought to be concentrated on trying to find the woman, dragging her out into the open?

It wasn't till she stood in the carpeted silence of the undertaker's, seeing probing gaze lighting on her fair hair, hearing a softly startled, "You wish to pay the expenses, madam?" that she realised what a fool she had been.

She shrank away from him. She simply couldn't help it, knowing that behind those rimless glasses his eyes were probing, his mind questioning the coming of a fair-haired woman to pay the funeral expenses of the dead girl.

Then he said, "They are already paid," the words over-riding the beginnings of her stammered explanation that she was an old friend of the Zamias'. His gaze dropped away from hers. "An envelope came this morning containing the cash and the request we use it for settling the account." He raised his gaze again. She fancied that in his eyes, in the words was a hint of warning. "Due to . . . out of the ordinary circumstances, we felt it our duty to hand the note to the police."

She stood there, simply staring at him. Conscience money, she thought shrinkingly. Money paid to still a conscience anguished by . . . what? The fact that she hadn't gone back and now knew the girl might have lived if she had; or because of a slap . . . a push . . . but whichever way, conscience money paid . . .

She said sharply, "Wasn't there any clue to the sender? I mean . . . you mentioned the police . . ." her voice trailed off.

"Nothing. Excepting of course, that the sender must be in the position to afford such a gesture."

She took another step back, sure now that there was warning in his eyes; that he was telling her to her face that she could be traced through that fact. His questing gaze seemed to go over her yellow suit, over her shoes and purse, appraising every penny they might have cost.

He said abruptly, rapidly, "As we informed the officers . . . as they knew themselves . . . it does occasionally happen that when a child dies, when the parents are in poor circumstances, the officiating undertakers receive a sum of money to help with expenses from some generous soul, but in this case . . ."

She turned, was walking to the door with the man at her side. She knew that her lips were moving, that her tongue was forming words of thanks, apologies for wasting his time. Only when someone bumped against her outside in the street did she become fully conscious again of anything.

And then it was of Eileen Zamia she thought—Eileen with her talk of a bill being sent . . .

Ring her? Tell her . . . her whole body and mind shrank from the thought of that aggressive voice, that bare-hidden hate. So . . . send a letter?

By messenger, she thought rapidly. Not by post. So that the woman would have it that afternoon and not ring the house again. And offer, she thought rapidly, to pay for a headstone too. There was triumph in that thought. She was going to stay just one step ahead of Eileen's demands if she could, so that the woman had no further chance to taunt her, probe at her again.

She went into the messenger service offices on the heels of the decision, scribbled the note, addressed it and gave it to the dull-eyed teenager behind the desk, then saw a spark of interest lighting the dullness.

"Zamia?" She jerked. "That's Carol's mum, isn't it?"

"Yes." On the point of turning away she swung back to the counter. "You knew Carol."

"Oh sure. I saw her Sunday. At Church that was. D'you know, the sermon was all about never knowing what the minute holds. You don't, do you? And we were all laughing at her after."

"Why?"

"Oh she was sounding off, playing Miss Big as usual. She had a radio at church—she was going somewhere after, and after service she was outside skiting she had some big secret and the radio was blab-it-not payment." She rolled her eyes dramatically. "We laughed. Gee, you never took much notice of Carol. But still, she's dead, isn't she."

75

Gabriel stood in the sunshine outside the messenger service offices and abruptly, without going back to the car, walked along the pavement to Phil's offices on the second floor of a new modernistic block that was more glass than brick, a place Phil wryly referred to as the goldfish bowl.

She met him at the top of the stairs, his grab at her, his quick hug, almost throwing her off balance. He said, before she could draw breath, "You were coming to invite me to lunch. Dear woman, I accept. What'll it be, pie and two veg. at the local, or spaghetti at the Itie place? Either way," he tucked her arm firmly in his, "we'll develop indigestion, but I refuse to eat in this place any more. I used to have to gulp sandwiches behind the desk, till I found out I was a peepshow to half the passers-by. Have you ever felt like a monkey, Angel? I did. All it needed was for them to throw me peanuts or a banana . . ."

"Phil," she resisted his efforts to draw her down the stairs again, "I want to talk to you."

"Coo, ducks," he pulled a clown face at her. "You sound like my dear old goose when she used to catch me raiding the biscuit tin." Then his smile died. He looked at her searchingly. He said quietly, "Something's wrong? Really wrong? All right, sweetheart, I'm here."

It was so like the old days, so like the boyish Phil who had soothed her childish hurts, always been there to comfort and protect when she was hurt, that her eyes filled with sudden absurd tears.

Silently she followed him back into the inner office, past the girl in the outer office who looked at them, bright-eyed, pert with curiosity. He let the venetian slats fall over the glass and in the privacy of that dim half-light, faintly green in its reflection through the slats, she was suddenly at a loss, so deep in memory of the old days that she felt tongue-tied, wanted to run away without putting the question.

But all it needed was a simple explanation, she told herself. Just a few words and a smile and the mountain she was making out of that lie, out of Carol's boastings on Sunday, would be finished.

76

She asked bluntly, "Phil, why did you lie to me? *You* gave that radio to Carol. Why lie to me?"

"So that's caught up with me." He spoke flatly, back to her, his fingers prying two of the slats aside, letting him peer out into the street. "But . . . remember when you asked me?" He turned to face her, half-smiling. "I said something about—did you think I'd grown into a dirty old man who gave presents to little girls—something along that line, and wow!" he pulled a little face, "you jumped down my throat with some talk of never thinking of that, that perhaps Carol's yarn of some chap molesting her was true, and the radio was the pay-off."

"Well?"

"Well, we went on talking of Carol's yarn, things like that, and Fred's betting. We never got back to who was the person who gave her the radio . . ."

"We did! You suggested that Fred's betting would have to pay off some time and Carol would benefit from the winnings, to the extent of that radio for instance and . . ."

"It was you who made that suggestion, Angel. I merely said Fred would have to win some time and Carol wouldn't have handed over her wages without some sort of agreement that she'd have a share in any wins . . . then, I remember it clearly . . . you retorted you were a dill," his clown smile was back, "that you hadn't thought of it, that a good win would buy the radio . . . and from there we slid on to other things."

Had they? She couldn't clearly remember at all. Hazily she groped in memory. She said, half-petulantly, "but why didn't you correct me? You left me with the impression . . . it was a lie of omission actually and . . ."

"You *are* on the warpath," he said lightly, lounging against the slatted window. "It didn't seem important. I only remembered about it later, and why the fuss?"

Her head jerked up. She said flatly, "Phil, it's absurd you should give a girl Carol's age a sixty-dollar radio. You know it is. And she told people she knew a wonderful secret and the radio was for keeping quiet about it. Now explain that!"

"Why should I?"

The harshness of his voice was something new, startling, and suddenly alarming. She sat there, staring at him in the faintly greenish half-light.

He said with that same harshness, "You're not my keeper, Angel Gabriel You've no right, have you," his tone was milder, "to demand I explain anything."

She felt her cheeks burning. Mutinously, much as she had met some rebuff of their childhood, when he'd refused to take her somewhere, let her do something, she said, "That's not fair." Then she added, "Though I admit you're right. I have no right, but . . . I'm going to worry. I won't be able to help it. What's wrong that you had to pay a girl like Carol sixty dollars? That's what it comes to, you know. Imagining things," she pressed on stubbornly, "is a darn sight worse than having the truth handed you, and you know it."

"Damn," he said softly. "And blast. And a few other things. You were always a wretchedly curious little beast, Angel Gabriel. You're going to worm and pry till you get hold of the story, aren't you? Perhaps even run to my nosey big sis, asking questions—getting *her* alarmed . . . well, I won't have it, understand? Oh, to hell with it . . . you might as well know, I expect. I won't have you scaring the daylights of Jericho out of Sis and the rest of the family . . ."

"I shan't run to May, or anyone else," she retorted indignantly.

"All right then. Carol found out something I didn't want made public. That's all there is to it. She didn't demand anything for keeping quiet. I explained the situation, pointed out facts, asked her to shut up. She liked me. She was willing. It wasn't anything criminal and honestly," the clown grin was back, "I never made a pass at her. Poor kid, I think she would have welcomed one. The boys ignored her, which must have been galling."

"How did she find out?"

"My fault. She was all the time harping on the subject, and one evening she said something about some chap always returning home about ten and how about that? And I snapped her down— told her she was up a gum tree, because of course Berry was alive long past that." He was abruptly silent.

78

"So it was to do with Bernice Strang? Phil, I asked if you knew her." She was suddenly frightened, while telling herself it was crazy. There was nothing to be frightened about. But, memory pressed, Phil had lied about Bernice too. She cried, "You said you'd met her in the toy shop and yet . . . I've heard you were enemies. You lied again. Why?"

He said wryly, "Another sin of omission. Call it that. Why should I have gone into explanations? Say that Berry Strang wished a pox on me. I liked her, you know, but she was a menace." At her startled look he laughed. "On the roads. She'd learned to drive in Africa. Goodness knows what sort of laws they have, what sort of roads. I guess she used to zoom along on deserted places how she liked. Her pappa, you know, was some education wallah over there. He had a heart attack. Curtains for pappa." His tone was half-mocking. "So they came over here. And Berry couldn't get it into her head that she should drive anyway different to the past. Oh, she was safe enough right in town—traffic's practically strangled there, anyway and you have to crawl. But out in the open . . . wow!" he raised his gaze to the ceiling. "I had one side-sweep from her—with all the building, subdividing, I was out in the open a lot. Then she crashed right into me one evening. She was all apologies—she had lots of charm and was a nice kid, but a menace. I told her as much, but she thought she could gloss it over with a few sweet words, an offer to settle the damage from her own pocket. I told her she needed a lesson—needed to learn how to drive out here. The upshot was she lost her licence for three months . . ."

"Was that why she had to walk home that night she was killed?" she asked quietly.

She was sure it wasn't the greenish half-light that made him seem so appalling white. He said, in a half-whisper, "She had no need to walk. I offered to drive her home."

"*You* did!"

He made an impatient movement and the venetian slats behind him rattled and were silent again. He said, "So I've let that out— you might as well know the rest. I was driving home late and I came across her and Nick."

79

"Nick!"

But of course Nicholas had lived here then, she thought confusedly. How funny that she'd never asked how long the pair had known one another. It was just something she had taken for granted—Nick knew Phil and that was that.

Now she asked, "How long have you known Nick?"

"Oh . . . eighteen months or so. Why? We were boarding in houses along the same street—my home had gone by then. And that night I met up with him and Berry. Nick's car had broken down—he was peeving all the way home I remember. I offered them a lift. Nick hopped in, but I knew she'd refuse. She said something about liking fresh air. I smelt, you see, ducks," he gave her a rueful clown-grin. "She pointedly said goodnight to Nick. Not to me. And marched off. And I laughed."

His expression, his face, reminded her of the girl who had spoken of laughing at Carol the last time they'd met.

She asked huskily, "Weren't you worried about her alone that way . . . I mean . . ."

He straightened. "Good grief, do you think I left her in the middle of nowhere? She was in the middle of a street. It was a fine night, with a warrior's shield moon. There were street lights, too. But I think that bastard came along only a little while later. She looked tired. He need only have called her by name . . ."

She jerked, "But this didn't come out. Did it?"

"No. Isn't that what I'm saying? Nick and I were green the next day when she was found, but what in blazes could we do? I never saw another soul that night. Neither did Nick. If we'd stepped forward we'd have been in a blaze of publicity, perhaps even suspected for a time, certainly harrassed by the police . . ."

She said harshly, "So you preferred to turn your face and go past on the other side the street, Phil? Didn't you condemn this unknown woman for just that?"

He said savagely, "*We'd* have been no help."

"This woman didn't know she could have been a help."

They gazed at one another in sharp mutual hostility while she

80

thought it was almost hysterically funny that Nick all this time had been hiding something, as she herself had been doing. But there was a vast difference, she thought wearily, between Nick's secret and her own. Nick's was simply . . . a sin of omission . . .

Phil was saying, "I explained it to Carol and she agreed to keep quiet. The radio—actually I didn't buy that and you can check if you're so inclined. I won it in a charity raffle at the pub. I didn't want it and Carol came into the office one afternoon just after I'd got the thing, started going pop-eyed over it and . . . well, I said she could have it."

"And what would you have done if she'd broken her promise?"

"Bro. . . ? Why should she have? She'd get nothing."

"Except a chance to appear important." She jerked out. "What if she'd told and people had suggested that you knew where Bernice Strang had walked that night and you . . . you might have dropped Nick at home . . . and driven back . . ."

His mouth smiled, but his eyes were watchful. He said lightly, "You have a horrible mind. Carol wouldn't have told and got herself into my bad books. Now come to lunch."

She stood up, shaking her head. "No. I have to get back."

He came towards her then. His hands, firm, gentle, rested on her shoulders, drawing her forward. His mouth touched hers and a flame of remembrance for past kisses, for a past way of life, was back. She drew back sharply. He made no comment on her shrugging withdrawal, only said, "Thank you, my love," half-mockingly.

To cover her embarrassment she started speaking, aimlessly, disjointedly, and then the words were neither aimless or disjointed at all. She was saying, "Phil, someone sent money to pay for Carol's funeral . . ."

And he was breaking in, "I know."

And the two of them were staring at one another again in that sharp hostility.

She demanded, "*How* did you know?"

"Because I sent it. Well, don't look so shocked," he added lightly. "It's not a crime, surely. In fact I felt downright virtuous. Oh stop staring!" he went on irritably. "Iley hasn't two pennies to rub together and Fred's no help with anything. I suppose the truth is I've always felt responsible for Iley ever since that confounded accident. It was my fault. You never knew that, did you? Do you know, I can't even remember now what it was she was ticking me off about, but I said 'Oh give over, Iley' and pushed her well aside out of what I was doing and she . . . it was downright funny in a way. You know how my dear old goose kept the floors like glass? Iley went skating away in a beautiful glide, with her mouth growing wider and wider in shock. And then she fell. The most humiliating bit of it to me was she didn't tell on me either. I'd have caught hell of course and she knew it, but oddly enough I'd rather she'd told."

"Because it put you under an obligation!" She was torn between indignation, irritation and plain amusement. "I can just picture Iley never letting you forget, but why on earth have you played up to her all this time?"

He grinned, but it didn't touch his eyes. They mocked at her, at the past, at the plans they'd made in the brief time of their engagement. "It rather tickled me having a family to watch over. Call it that."

"Did she ask you to pay for the funeral?"

"No. I did that off my own bat."

"Why? And why the secrecy? Why send the money, with no name, no word . . ."

"Because I didn't want Iley to find out who'd paid it. As soon as she knows she'll be down there harrassing the undertakers, but I'm damned if I'm getting involved in an emotional scene with Iley bawling buckets all over me." His eyes were reflective. "But how come you know all about it?"

There was only one answer that wouldn't cause trouble. She avoided his searching gaze as she said, "Because I went down to pay for it. I . . . well, like you, I know she hasn't two pennies to rub together . . . and she's pregnant and . . . and Carol's death was so . . . well anyway, I went."

He gave a sudden grunt of laughter. "What paragons we are!"

She said rapidly, "But you'll have to admit it, Phil, because . . . they took the note . . . to the police!" As he jerked upright she went on tightly, "They think it's from the running woman, of course—that she's salving her conscience by trying to help with the expences."

After a moment he shrugged it aside. "Well let them. It doesn't matter, and it might make the district feel more kindly towards her."

"But it won't! Can't you see the money's utterly condemning her! It's the last straw! It's . . . well, it's as good as having her say that she knows she's in the wrong; that it's all true—that she ran away, not wanting to be involved, or else she smacked Carol for some reason—if she comes forward now and tries to say she never ever saw Carol, that a snake frightened her . . . something like it . . . and it could be true for all we know . . . she won't be believed. The money's making the other story, or stories, look quite true . . ."

"Which is better than having people put two and two together and make sixteen hundred!" he said crisply. "Stop gobbling at me, Gabriel and listen to sense. You've admitted in your actions, your own questions, that you've heard this dreamed-up trash that Carol knew something of Berry's death. In your heart of hearts you must know it's certainly pure poison, started by someone eager for sensation. Carol simply tripped on that bridge and fell and that's all there is to it. Can't you imagine what it will be like if talk goes on? If this tale of Carol being mauled by some man is dragged into light? Every man who ever had anything to do with either girl will find his life hell. Isn't it far better to let everyone believe that woman paid for the funeral? That she's done her best to make some sort of amends? The talk about Berry will die down." He touched her shoulders with his hands, pressed down, gave her a little shake. He reminded, "I asked you before to leave this wretched business alone. Why can't you?"

She tried to speak lightly, to make a mock of it, "Because I'm young and fair and as you said yesterday fingers are pointing . . . I . . . don't like it."

Her mind urged, Tell him. Everything, but she knew she wouldn't. She was going to wait—just a little while longer, she told herself. A day, two days, three . . . such a lot could happen.

The woman could be found, or come forward and she'd never have to see suspicion slide into Phil's eyes, and perhaps stay there.

She thought wearily, And even if I tell him, what can he do? That I haven't done myself?

CHAPTER NINE

"Are you calling your fair lady?"

Her plump body filled the doorway as she stood with one hand on cushioned hip, one behind her blonde hair.

"Oh, come off it, Bet," he grinned absently, "We all know if you'd been on the creek path Mrs. Buchanan would've thought she was seeing Siamese twins or the backside of an elephant." Expertly he dodged the tea-towel. "Come off it, love, this is serious. I've remembered something and I don't care for it." At her raised brows he said anxiously, "I remember who that woman was. The one I saw getting off the bus. It's Sturt's cousin—the one who married Endicott. No, hush a tick—you just listen. I remember her from years back. A skinny little bit of a thing without much to say for herself. I remember clear as yesterday the time there was some Sunday School treat on . . . she'd have been about sixteen or seventeen then. She used to help teach. They hired two coaches that time to go down the coast and roped me in as driver for one . . . remember that? I said, making conversation, I supposed this girl was going to help with the ones that wanted to go in the water.

"She turned brick red and her mum chimed in and said the girl had some rheumatic condition. She wasn't allowed in swimming and couldn't swim come to that. I remember thinking the girl looked a bit of a baby and her mum ought to let her grow up. The point is—you think she's grown up since and learned to swim?"

He drew a deep breath, "And don't tell me to go ask. Or ask Sturt either. Or tell him that she was hopping off a bus here Monday all tricked up in white. If there's nothing fishy about that she's told him. If she hasn't . . ."

She looked down at her hands, picking absently at a piece of flaking polish on her thumb.

She said flatly, "You just go sell beer and forget about it."

"*Now* you tell me!" He threw up his hands. "And ever since

85

Tuesday it's been nag, nag, who was she? And telling me I ought to remember because it could be important because a lot of innocent women were going to have their lives investigated by every nosey cow in the district. Now didn't you? And when I do remember you say forget it."

"I didn't say forget it for good," she gave back tartly. "You just keep quiet till one of the police drop in for a beer and then say casual-like that you'd been wracking your brains over the woman you'd seen and you'd now remembered it was Mrs. Endicott and ha-ha-ha wasn't it a laugh you'd bothered, as it couldn't be her, could it, who was the running woman? That way there'll be no hard feelings if there's nothing in it."

. . .

Gabriel went on sitting there long after she'd replaced the receiver. Her gaze was towards the aviary. She could hear bird voices, see them fluttering, but she wasn't conscious of any of it. It was the second call she'd had that evening. The first she'd almost managed to dismiss from her mind, though at the time there'd been first fear, then blazing anger, then contempt, because the breathless voice had merely said, when she'd spoken, "Where were you on Monday evening, Mrs. Endicott? On the Larapinta Bridge?" and then the line had gone dead.

At first thought had questioned, Was I seen? then anger had prompted, of course not. This was someone who's come under suspicion striking out at someone else. Contempt had finished it with, Words and insinuations won't get them anywhere. They've no proof.

But now . . .

She could remember every word Lisa Buchanan had spoken.

The voice had been crisp, almost as though the woman hadn't wanted to phone; had forced herself to the action, and wanted to get it over as quickly as possible.

"The police have come to me, Mrs. Endicott," she had said, "They asked me—was this woman perhaps dressed in a white suit? A long-sleeved white suit with straight jacket, straight skirt, and tan-coloured shoes. A purse, too. And dark binding round the front of the jacket."

Somehow she had managed to force her tongue into the necessary words, "Do they know who the woman is then?"

"No. They said not."

She had drawn a long slow painful breath of relief; then had wondered if the woman could hear it across the line. She had said, "Then it doesn't help. Does it?" and had wondered then why the woman had chosen to ring her.

"Perhaps not. I thought I would tell you. Because . . . they asked if I knew you—had met you—had ever seen you. They didn't say why."

Again the line had simply gone dead, but this time fear didn't give way to anger and contempt. It remained fear and went on growing.

But it's ridiculous, she told herself. They can't say I had anything to do with it. Even if they did, this woman would come forward. Wouldn't she?

Thought questioned bluntly, Why should she? She thinks she's safe, hidden from trouble. Why should she bother her head about some other woman?

Fear came back, stroked coldly at her throbbing temples, making her jerk upright, shivering, when the door bell pealed. Rang again when she didn't answer and went on ringing, reminding her of the previous evening and her call on Miss Traill.

It seemed a parody of her actions when there was a voice calling to her from the half-open window. "Gabriel!" it said, "It's Phil."

She moved then, called, "I'm coming," and went flying to the front door, throwing it open, seeing only blurred shapes for a moment because of the dusk outside. Then she realised there were three people; realised it and shrank back as Phil's voice said, "The police want to talk to you, Gabriel," and he stepped forward.

The surprise in her voice was quite real. In spite of Lisa Buchanan's phone call, of what she'd said, she was still honestly surprised that the police should be there, that Phil should be saying so in such a grave voice, and her voice rang sharp with surprised question, "The police?" and began to ask, "But why should . . ." and then trailed away because she saw his eyes.

She might have been looking at Miss Traill, at Lisa Buchanan, at the man in the undertaker's. All the speculation, the wonder, the suspicion was mirrored there, in Phil's own eyes.

Abruptly she turned away. She led the way silently back into the long room, gestured to chairs, asked, "What do you want?"

. . .

"How absurd." Her voice seemed now to be coming from a distance, tinny and echoing to her own ears. "Oh, I quite admit I can't swim. But . . . well, how absurd to say I could be that running woman."

The policemen were solid-looking and young. She hadn't heard their names. They were simply policemen. One was quite silent. The other was staring at her with wide, guileless-looking brown eyes and saying, "Well, you're fair, you see. And young." The guileless-seeming gaze went over her thoughtfully. "And we're told that on Monday evening you were wearing a white dress."

"A cream suit," she corrected.

"Is that so?" His gaze expressed innocent dismay. "I'll just alter that."

She could hear the minutes ticking away on the wall clock and then suddenly they were drowned under the birdsong as the birds, frightened into silence by strangers, came alive again.

But the policeman didn't seem to notice them. He went on pulling out a notebook, and slowly turning the leaves, finding a pencil and slowly writing.

Her mind warned her that he was trying to prick at her nerves, make her rush into speech to break the silence. Guileless, she thought wretchedly. He was about as guileless as a bull with a deceptively gentle face.

"Well now," he said brightly at last, "You wore a cream suit. To visit friends in Larapinta would that be?"

He still hadn't told her where she'd been seen. The question

88

fretted mercilessly at nerves and thought as she answered, "I went into the city. Shopping."

"Buy a lot?" he suggested and for a minute she was deluded by the pleasantness of his voice. Just in time she remembered that the running woman couldn't have been burdened with parcels and she nearly lied. Only the remembrance that she'd been seen, somewhere in Larapinta, saved her from the stupidity.

She shook her head.

"And you decided to visit friends on the way home perhaps, in Larapinta?"

Again the swift decision—lies or truth. It had to be the latter, she realised helplessly. He's soon find out there was no visit, no friends to back her up.

"No."

She realised in childish triumph that her simple answers were giving him nothing to grip on. He glanced from her to Phil. She had only dared to glance at him once and then the sight of his compressed lips had made her turn away.

The policeman rubbed down the buttons of his uniform jacket with one hand. He said, "You didn't go straight home though?"

"No."

"You left the bus in Larapinta?" he pressed.

"Yes."

"Why?"

"Really," strength, determination, the ability to think, were sweeping back, echoed in her assured, "I feel that's hardly any of your business."

Phil said sharply, "Don't be a fool, Gabriel."

Her gaze flickered towards him and away. In that moment she disliked him intensely, even hated him. How dare he, she thought furiously, look at me with suspicion?

She said crisply, "Then . . . embarrassing to admit, I left the bus because I simply had to go to the ladies' room."

She saw the disconcerted expression on the young face opposite and added, "I didn't mean to get off there. I bought a ticket straight through to Paltara. I should think you could check that. But in Larapinta . . . well . . ." she shrugged, smiled.

The policeman coughed. He asked, "And so you went on home by the next bus?"

"I'm not certain. Embarrassing to admit again, but frankly I had a frightful stomach ache. Something I'd eaten in the city I expect. I don't know whether I caught the next one, or the one after that."

"You went into the hotel, I expect?"

Her hesitation was brief. In the hotel there might have been people about who could call her a liar, she remembered. She said, "No. Into the public place between the two shops just down from the bus stop."

She knew she had said the wrong thing. Panic came welling back, was visible she knew, in her shaking hands. He said pleasantly, "That's easy to check. The council has a full-time attendant on there now to stop the vandalism."

He applied himself to his notebook again. The birds went on singing and the minutes ticked away while she wondered, rubbing her sweating hands gently together, whether to admit to the lie or stay silent.

Then he shot at her, so suddenly that she gasped, "Why did you offer to pay the girl's funeral expenses, Mrs. Endicott?"

She knew her hesitation was far too long, that when she did manage to speak the words sounded quite unconvincing, "I used to know the family. Mrs. Zamia that is. Before her marriage. I didn't connect up the name at first. When I did I went out to see them to . . . well, to say just how sorry I was about it. I thought . . . well it was simply a gesture I suppose, of . . . politeness. They . . . they seemed so . . . badly off, and I had money of my own . . ."

"You haven't seen them since her marriage—how long ago would that be?" he broke in.

"Fifteen years. I remember . . ." she stopped, realised she'd been trapped into a foolish admission and reddened.

"Fifteen years." He spaced out each syllable, so that the words sounded appallingly wrong. "So after fifteen years you go to see them and are so sorry . . . Mrs. Endicott, why did you give Mrs. Zamia a cheque, too?"

She couldn't answer. Or look at Phil.

He said, "Her husband changed it this morning in the hotel. That's how we know."

She managed at last, "I told her to buy something for the coming baby. It is expected soon."

"Very generous of you," he commented. His expression said, "Surely unbelievably generous of you."

He ran his hand down his tunic buttons again. "Mrs. Endicott, you went to see Mrs. Buchanan, didn't you?"

"Yes."

"Why?"

"About the pool. I wanted her to come and talk to people. To . . . to make them see how easy it was for . . . for a tragedy to happen . . . for . . ."

"You went twice?"

"Yes."

"You asked a lot of questions about the running woman though, didn't you?"

She said defiantly, "It's the topic of the district. Of course I was curious about it. Doubly so because I'm fair and was dressed in white on Monday."

"You were by the creek too?" he shot at her.

"No!"

The denial came violently.

He said, "You asked a lot of questions about Bernice Strang, too, didn't you?"

"Well . . . we got talking of that. Carol was . . . playing detective, so far as I can make out."

"A rather silly sort of girl, you'd say?"

"I expect so. I don't know. I only know what people have told me of her."

He nodded, watching her as he said, "You seem to have gone out of your way to find out all you could about her. You asked Mr. Brown a lot of questions, didn't you? You seemed very interested in her, even down to how much money she might have had to play with. Isn't that so?" he shot at her.

Again the hesitation was too long, she knew. She blurted out at

91

last, "I wanted to know how the family was placed. I thought . . . they might be in difficulties . . . without her money and . . ."

It sounds ridiculous, she thought frantically. Of course he thinks, and knows, that what I'm saying is ridiculous.

He pointed the fact out to her with a swift, "And yet you hadn't seen anything of Mrs. Zamia for fifteen years . . . since you were a bit of a girl?" He didn't wait for a reply, but went on, "You seemed very interested in the way Carol was prying into Bernice Strang's death, too."

She said flatly, "I was curious. Who wouldn't be? The girl had been saying she had a clue about it . . ."

"Did you think that was the truth?"

"No!" she denied sharply. "She seemed to have been the sort of silly child who made up fantastic ideas . . . why," her voice grew stronger, "one of her teenage friends told me no one paid any attention to her—she was always making up stories to get into the limelight. They laughed . . ."

He seemed to have lost interest in the point. He was looking down at his notebook. He said, without looking up, "Were you surprised when you heard the funeral had been paid for?"

"Yes, of course I was," she agreed eagerly. "Very surprised. But I know now who paid for it. It wasn't the running woman as I thought at first—a sort of . . . conscience-easing payment you know. It was Phil," her gaze flickered up to him and away again. "He's known the family all these years. He knew they couldn't afford the funeral so he paid for it, without saying who'd sent the money, so they wouldn't be embarrassed—overwhelm him with gratitude—that sort of thing. He told me about it straight after I'd been to the funeral parlour. I told him, you see, that . . ."

He nodded. "Oh yes, the undertaker told us he'd seen you go to Mr. Sturt's offices. That's how he knew who you were. He went in and asked the office girl in there."

Nasty, sneaking little wretched man, she thought in furious anger, so that his next words washed over her before she had a chance to be prepared to meet further trouble.

"He showed his suspicions of you, didn't he, Mrs. Endicott? So that you got frightened and ran off to Mr. Sturt and suggested to him that he should say he'd made the payment, if anyone asked. Isn't that so?"

"Why . . . oh, how utterly *mad*!" she croaked.

Phil said remotely, "I've told you the simple truth. I paid the money. Mrs. Endicott made no suggestions of any kind to me about it."

She had never known till then that a silence could express disbelief far more plainly than any words. She was trembling with sick fear and anger together when he began again, "Carol Zamia was a silly sort of girl. She was fond of adding two and two together and making a hundred. She thought herself a detective and was claiming she had a clue to the death of Bernice Strang. You're with me so far?" he asked softly.

She nodded.

He asked, quite mildly, "Now would that clue have had something to do with your husband and Mr. Sturt, Mrs. Endicott?"

She simply went on staring at him.

"Would it have been the fact that on the night Miss Strang died your husband and your cousin were seen with her?"

She glanced upwards, at Phil, then away. He was staring remotely over her head, at the fluttering birds, as though he'd withdrawn himself completely from what was happening.

The policeman said, quite pleasantly, "Oh yes, Mrs. Endicott, we know about it. Officially the Strang case was closed a long, long time ago. The man concerned is dead. You didn't know, did you? No one did, of course, because it's not official habit to pillory the family of an insane man who can't be made to account for what he's done. So, there was official silence about it. It was a long time after the case closed we had an anonymous letter about your husband and Mr. Sturt. We did nothing about it. There was no point in doing so. Mrs. Endicott," he shot at her abruptly, "You've been ill, haven't you?"

"Ill?" She simply stared, then shook her head violently, "No."

"Distressed, then? So that you've shut yourself off from friends, acquaintances? Kept to this house?"

"I've been widowed," she said flatly. "Isn't it quite natural that . . ."

"Yes, widowed. You hadn't known your husband long, had you? And you were only married a short time—a bare month or so?"

When she didn't answer, he asked, "Mrs. Endicott, did you love your husband?"

With a cold dignity that tried to hide angry bewilderment, she demanded, "Have you any right to ask me that?"

He shrugged. "Would you agree his death was a terrible shock? That . . ."

She leaned forward. She said bitterly, "Wouldn't you call it a terrible shock that could see somebody . . . close to you . . . drive away into the night and an hour later a voice would tell you the person was dead . . . and you were taken to a cold little room, and made to look at . . . him . . . and know . . ." she was shivering violently.

"So you'll agree it was quite enough to stretch your nerves to breaking point? So that for a while afterwards you wouldn't be quite . . . normal? So that if a stupid youngster in search of sensation tried to make out the person you'd lost, were grieving for still, had had something to do with a horrible murder, you might be quite likely to lose your head, strike out, hit the youngster . . .

"Mrs. Endicott, did it happen that way on the bridge? Did Carol Zamia recognise you and say something to you connecting your dead husband with Miss Strang? So that you were violently angry and upset, slapped her? So that she fell, into the creek, and you couldn't get her out again?"

CHAPTER TEN

"You actually paid the Zamias off? With a cheque? With some thing they can wave as proof you've been paying to keep them quite, quite silent? Little jumping lizards, my angel dill!"

The old childish mockery was in the voice; the words were ones he might have used years ago when they were small, but it was a stranger's gaze that looked searchingly into her own.

He added, "The story's all over town, I'm afraid. It was the landlord of the Larapinta pub who saw you on Monday. He only remembered who you were when Fred Zamia went in there to cash your cheque over the bar. When he remembered your name he let it out in front of everyone in the place. He saw you, in white leaving the bus . . ."

"I've explained that." The words came thickly. "They can't prove I'm a liar. That policeman tried to trick me." Indignation only thickened her voice still more. The words were slurred, odd-sounding as she went on, "There's no attendant in that place at all. I remember reading in the local paper that the council said no to having someone, because of the big expense of wages and . . . all that . . . the policeman . . . dreadful . . . tricky . . ." the words slurred off into a tangle of sound.

Phil's clown face was old suddenly, old and tired. He came close to her, his hand touching her shoulder, pressing down, "Do you realise that the cheque is proof, to the police, that you were trying to ease a very guilty conscience? You hadn't seen Iley for fifteen years and yet here you are . . . trying to pay for the funeral into the bargain. My office girl told me the undertaker had bounced in and questioned her about you. When she told me later and I thought about you, your fair hair, what suspicions the wretched fool of a man might have, I thought it was best to go to the police."

95

He shrugged. "And a fat lot of good I did. They're perfectly convinced we cooked that story up between us. They kept me there for a couple of hours, walking round and round the whole situation . . ."

She burst out, "Isn't the fact I went there the very proof I'm not this woman? If I was why on earth would I show myself there and ask . . ."

"They'll think you went there to make sure the money had come. That you're so shaken up you don't realise half of what you're doing. The undertaker is having a merry time swearing himself blue that you nearly passed out when he told you he'd informed the police, and that you were desperate to find out if there was some clue in the envelope to the sender. He considered that was why you came to him—to find out if you were still safe, or if you'd slipped up somewhere."

She said, "He's lying. I must have looked . . . surprised. Wouldn't you have been surprised? And then I *hoped* there was some clue to the sender. He's as sensation-minded as Carol is supposed to have been. He's making things up . . ."

"Do you think he's the only one? Oh, Angel," now he might have been speaking to her eight-year-old self who had failed to understand one of their childish ploys. "Rumour's sitting up and taking nourishment and any minute it's going to hop out of bed and run hooting down the street in fine fettle. The police can't sit back and say, 'lordy, lordy, what a noise the dear creature makes, to be sure', and put their pinkies in their ears. They're going to have to pop outdoors, bring rumour in, give it a chair and take the story down in triplicate. And there it is—you knew Carol. She could have stopped you on the bridge, said something abominable about Nick—and you slapped her. She fell. And you can't swim.

"The police won't be able to wipe it off as a simple accident as they'd have done in the first place if you'd come forward. Rumour's gone too far and too many women have been slandered . . ."

"They can't touch me," she said defiantly.

"No? At the very least it'll be unpleasant. For God's sake stop fooling yourself! You'll be asked eventually was it accident, or a

96

deliberate shove? It's no good opening your mouth and staring at me with saucer eyes. Gabriel, you have to face it that it's quite likely you'll have a manslaughter charge slapped on to you. I don't know exactly how the law would look at it, but the fact is you hit the wretched girl, and she died."

She managed, "I'm not the running woman." When he didn't say anything, only turned away from her, she babbled, "I've been thinking, over and over . . . don't you see, she could be a total stranger to the district? Quite a lot of people, especially women, like to look over new houses, alone, without an agent at their elbow urging them to sign up. What if she was a foreigner, who knew little English, was scared of the police? She might easily have run right away . . ."

The frightfulness of the thought washed over her in misting waves of panic. The idea that the woman could now have merged into some district miles and miles away, never to come forward and reveal herself, was terrifying.

She realised in astonishment that the room had taken on a queer appearance, as though mist had crept in through the windows, which was absurd. She wanted to ask if autumn could bring a thick, wavery fog like that and why the windows hadn't been shut, and then Phil was holding her tightly and she was asking, as though they were children again, "How am I going to get clear of this? What will I say? And do?"

He simply looked at her for a moment. Then the fighter of dragons of their childhood, the solver of problems, was simply saying in a leaden voice, "I haven't the faintest idea. Have you?" which was somehow completely shocking and unreal.

His hold on her slackened. He pressed her back on the gold-coloured cushions of the couch. He said quietly, "Listen to me. I can stand anything but you lying to me, so don't lie. No," one hand touched her mouth, "don't repeat the lie that you're not this woman. Could there be two women, both young, both fair, both dressed in white on a stormy autumn evening, both by the creek about the same time, both given to panic, both . . . oh no, it's not possible, is it? There's this, too—if you spill the whole thing now it's possible we could get it hushed up.

"No . . . wait," his fingers brushed her lips lightly again. "Iley's not going to tell the truth at the inquest, for one. Can't you see how the press would howl over her pitiful blackmailing? She'll turn up draped in black, with Kleenex tissues dropping behind her like snowflakes—the perfect, tear-sodden mamma and play it as gently as possible. After all you know, twenty-four dollars is an absurd sum of money. You could hardly call it blackmail and why hand out such an odd sum as silence money? It's the sort of cheque that might be handed over to pay the gas bill, between one friend and another who's a bit short.

"And then . . . you've been a widow for three months, Gabriel . . . three months isn't long. You could be pregnant."

"Pregnant?" she jerked and didn't know whether to laugh or cry or rage at him. "I'm not. What on earth . . ."

"Oh hush, hush," he might again have been speaking to the child Gabriel. "Hush up and use your brains. An expectant mamma is notoriously slightly wacky. A doctor's certificate you were expecting, on top of still suffering from shock over losing Nick . . . good lord, we could even claim you blacked out and when you came round . . ." his eyes were narrowed, bright with eagerness. "There's a perfect out, Angel. The wretched girl falls in. You run for help, but the effort's too much and you collapse. The rain starts and bring you round. You might have forgotten . . . it's not impossible . . . under the stress and shock, what you're doing there. You stagger home and afterwards you naturally can't admit the truth."

He said after a little, "If we think hard enough we can improve on that story. I'm sure of it. There's old McGinnis for a start. Practically retired, but he saw us both through cuts and bruises and measles and what have you. What's more likely you'd go to someone you knew and trusted if you were pregnant? I'm pretty sure he'd help . . . and look, I've heard plenty of cases where a witness doesn't appear. A statement is handed in and she's referred to as Mrs. X. If we had a medical certificate to say any more shock and strain for you might be the end . . . if McGinnis will agree. . . ."

It was calm, certain assumption that she was lying, that she was

98

really the running woman of Monday that made her blaze at him bitterly.

"I won't agree to that lie, or any other lie," she jerked away from him, rose to her feet, went to stand, leaning against the far wall, watching him. "Do you think, anyway, that someone . . . some clerk in the police station . . . some nosey reporter after a good story . . . wouldn't get hold of my name? Don't you know enough of human curiosity to know how it would be? People would never stop questioning and prying till they knew. Do you think women are going to sit back and have others think *they're* Mrs. X, the witness who wasn't named, who . . ."

She choked into shivering silence.

Phil asked, quite gently, "Are women unkind to each other? To another who's expecting a baby? Wouldn't they let the whole story die . . ."

Her mouth twisted. "Do you know the favourite occupation of a certain type of woman? Counting the months! When there's a wedding and a baby soon after you'll find them busy counting the months and expecting the worst and . . . they'd count the months and when they proved me a liar about the baby they'd prove me a liar about Carol's death. You didn't think of that, did you?" There was an absurd triumph in that moment, a pitiful triumph that died in a despairing, "It would all start again—all the speculation and questions—did Carol fall, or was she pushed? They'd say it was the latter because I lied to avoid appearing." She pressed shaking hands to her mouth. Through the guarding fingers her voice wailed, "Why should I be driven away from my home? From everything Nick built up? I'd have to go . . . and it's a lie. All of it."

Her hands dropped. She said savagely, "We've got to find that woman! You've got to find her for me, Phil! Please!"

His voice mocked, "Where do I start, Gabriel? And where do I finish? Here, in this room? With you?"

CHAPTER ELEVEN

It was the phone that finally dragged her from sleep. Even when her eyes were open, when she was really hearing the shrill sound, she couldn't fully focus on what it was, even where she was herself, or what it was that had to be faced.

If the ringing had stopped she might have fallen back on the pillows and gone back to sleep, she felt so drugged with exhaustion, but she couldn't stand the noise. Still in the nylon nightgown, rubbing her eyes open, she padded bare-footed into the long living-room.

Phil's voice asked, "Were you asleep?"

She asked in amazement, "Did you ring to ask me that? You woke me up."

"I thought . . . I just wanted to know if you were all right. I'll be up later on. Soon. Stay inside till I come up."

"But I can't do that." She was irritated at his stupidity and it showed in the impatience of her voice. "There are people I have to talk to. I should have seen Mrs. Brown before this. I thought there was no point because Mrs. Zamia said quite definitely Carol had turned down the delivery job, but don't you see that just because Carol didn't deliver the toys doesn't mean she and Mrs. Brown never met at all, and there's . . ."

"Do you think she'd talk to you, Gabriel?"

"She'd have to. Or to the police."

"And what do you think she'd say to the police? What do you think they'd even bother to ask her, come to that?" he demanded brutally. "And do you think anyone's going to answer your questions? They'll simply say 'she's out to throw suspicion on me or my friends or this woman or that, and I won't be party to it'."

She said sharply, "There are hundreds of people here in Paltara, or Larapinta who know me better than that. They know . . ."

"That you've shut yourself up like a nun for the past three

months, Gabriel. That's what they know. They know you're young and fair-haired and were in Larapinta on Monday, dressed in white, and that you tried to pay for that funeral . . . stop trying to fool yourself, Gabriel. And stay inside. *I'll* ask what questions I can, do what I can."

Act normally, her mind told her. Shut right out of thought what people might be saying, and act normally. Do the things you always do. So what to do first?

She moved sluggishly to the bathroom, to splash her face with water, then to the bedroom to slip into a housecoat, run a comb through her hair, and then move to the service hatch by the front door, all the time refusing to think of people talking, whispering, speculating.

Instead she thought of the absurdity of the previous evening, when, herself exhausted, and Phil looking deadly tired, he had forced her to bed, tucked her up as though she was still a child and had then asked, a frown of worry behind his dark brows, "Did you put out the milk bottle?"

Yet she hadn't been able to laugh at the ridiculous bit of normality intruding into tragedy, because she had numbly wondered how long it would be before forgetting or remembering the nightly milk bottle was of major importance again.

Her hand on the service door clasp, she glanced through the glass panels of the front door, and her hand became still. For a moment she simply wondered what was happening. Then a car came speeding along the road. Instantly they turned—still, watchful figures coming to life, turning eager faces towards the approaching car, turning again, disappointed faces watching it go, then turning full face towards the house again, watching stolidly—a boy on a bike, two women with shopping baskets, an old man, two teenage girls, three women with a cluster of children.

As she watched, another woman joined them. No one spoke. They simply waited.

For me to come out, she thought in shrinking disgust. For the police to come. For anything at all to happen.

She wondered what they would do if she did go out. Simply move aside? Or would they—horrible, impossible thought—press round her, taking in every feature of her appearɑnce, storing it up for later gossiping?

She thought of photos she'd seen in the press, and reports she'd read of crowds waiting outside courts for a glimpse of accused people; of other crowds standing through hours of simple watching of a house where there'd been some sensational happening.

No wonder Phil had told her to stay inside, she thought bitterly and tried to imagine what would happen if she ventured into the town; into the shops.

Deliberately she moved round the house, letting the venetian slats fall into place over the windows, shutting out light and the outside world, till the house had an eerie dimness. It was what she had done when Nicholas had died, she remembered.

Thinking back over those months of her brooding, her nun-like existence as Phil had called it, she could see how they could react against her. People, the police, Phil, everyone would say, "she hasn't been acting normally. She was strange. She withdrew from everyone." The right sort of atmosphere in fact to turn her into a nerve-wracked creature who might very well strike out at a child who said something against a dead man—a loved man.

Only I didn't love him, she thought wretchedly. Or his dream house. I've been . . . frightened of it.

That was it, she thought wearily. Frightened. Frightened of its perfection, fearing she couldn't live up to it, would disappoint Nicholas.

She'd never dared to alter one thing in it, for fear of annoying him, and after his death she'd gone on in the same way, carefully replacing each tiny figurine, each ornament, each cushion or piece of furniture in the same spot after she'd dusted and cleaned.

A sudden fury against its showroom perfection, an urge for action of any sort at all, made her run back to the bedroom, slip into slacks and shirt and move round the house, altering, disarranging, turning room after room from its perfection, trying to impress her own personality on the whole hated place.

When at last she fell, quite exhausted, on the living-room couch, she stared round in appalled fascination. The place wasn't a showroom any more—it wasn't anything, except a higgledy-piggledy collection of furniture, a draggled disorder. The pieces of furniture stood like so many blank-faced, out-of-place watchers . . .

The word brought her to her feet again. She went slowly back to the front door, peering through the slats across the glass there. The little crowd had altered only in the faces. There were still shopping baskets, now on different arms; still children, now with other young women; still a few teenagers; another young boy . . .

And Phil, she saw.

He was driving in, parking right outside the front door. The crowd was stirring, pressing towards the front fence. She wondered how long it would be before someone ventured inside the gate, came right up to the house, pressed their face to the glass . . .

She burst out, as she half-pulled him inside, "Those people! There were others at first, and now these! Just standing there. Staring!"

He said, "There's no harm in staring, Angel. A cat can look at a king."

She pressed her knuckles to her mouth, asked mumblingly, "What are they *saying*?"

He didn't answer. He was staring round the disordered living-room. He went on staring for a long time, then he went out the further door. She could hear him, walking through the whole house. She went running after him. She cried hysterically, "I hated it! Do you understand? I hated the place! It was Nick's dream house and I loathed it, and . . ." her voice calmed. She finished wearily, "I wanted to try and alter it."

Then she demanded, "Did you see Mrs. Brown? What are people *saying*? Have the police . . ."

He took her arm, let her back to the living-room, pushed her down on the couch, piled cushions behind her back. "Will you listen? Very carefully? You have until tomorrow. I've scraped that amount of grace out of them. They grudged it in one way. Were relieved in another, because if they get a statement from you, voluntarily, it's going to save a lot of trouble. You do understand, don't you?"

"No," she said flatly.

"Then I'll put it baldly. They're coming to see you at ten o'clock tomorrow. They're going to question you. What you say then is important. If you give a simple statement of an accident they'll accept your word and leave things for the inquest to cope with."

She said, "I'm not the running woman. You're asking me to admit to a lie—to . . . crucify myself. That's all it amounts to."

"You'll be crucified all right if you don't admit it," he told her brutally. "They'll want to know why you won't say what happened? They'll think there's something you desperately have to hide. On Monday, if you haven't made a sensible statement, a full-scale investigation will start. It won't be pleasant. It won't stop till every scrap of your life is turned upside down and inside out. Now . . . what are you going to say to the police in the morning? Think carefully . . ."

"I don't need to. I'll tell them I'm not the woman. That I never saw Carol Zamia. Never set eyes on her in my life."

He moved away from her. He said distantly, as though trying to withdraw himself from her and what the future held, "Then you'd better draw up some sort of statement of exactly what you . . . you're supposed," the inflexion on the word was slight, but still definitely there, "to have done on Monday.

"I'll take you over it, step by step, so there'll be no apparent flaws. First thing in the morning, if you still want to give that same statement, we'll go over it with a solicitor and at ten o'clock hand it to the police."

• • •

Phil said, "Yes, it *is* important. Every little bit of that Monday's important. You'll have to realise they're going to turn every why and wherefore into a dozen questions till they've drained you dry. Now start again. You were coming back from town. Why? It must be the first time since Nick's death that . . ."

She said, "You were always nagging at me. Go out. Stop being a vegetable. Stop brooding. You soon have to take over Nick's work. At the weekend I decided I'd make the first effort—go into town. Move round among people again. I didn't want to start with people I knew—people who'd stop and talk. I just wanted . . . to feel part of a crowd again. I went. I came back on the bus . . ."

"And got out at Larapinta. Why do that? When you'd booked through to Paltara? And you'll have to think of something better than that stomach ache."

"I can't tell you, because I don't know. The bus stopped. The driver called 'Larapinta'. I looked out the window and saw a signpost too and . . . my seat was just by the back door. I got out on impulse. Nothing more."

"And then you started towards the creek. Why?"

"Impulse again. Killing time. I didn't want to come back to the empty house. It isn't important. What is . . . Phil, I've been thinking—there are quite a few stretches of that path where there are no bends—just a straight stretch you can see along for quite a distance. Carol must have been well ahead of me or I'd have seen her somewhere. She couldn't have been behind me, or I'd have met her when I turned and came back. Don't you see that?" she asked eagerly, "and then . . ."

"If she was ahead of you why didn't you hear the splash as she fell? Hear her cry out? The sound of her struggling?"

She thought; offered, "For one thing I didn't go right up to the bridge, though I should think . . ." she fell silent, wondering how clearly sound would carry. Probably a long way on a still brooding evening like that Monday, she reflected. So she should have heard a cry, the splashing and churning of water.

Phil probed, "And the running woman? You didn't see her? Hear *her* cry out?"

"No."

"You can see for yourself that that's impossible, can't you?" he said quietly. "If Carol was well ahead of you and fell in before you came along you should have come face to face with that woman somewhere on the path as you walked forward and she rushed back."

It took her a long time to cope with that point. Finally she said lamely, "I didn't meet her coming. She didn't catch up with me as

I turned back. Phil, it *had* to happen long before I even set foot on the path, that's all!"

"Oh yes? And the boy? Mark? Sitting on the creek bank? Do you see anyone crediting him doing nothing about hearing cries, or seeing a woman rushing along . . ."

"Impossible again, of course," she tried to speak lightly, but her voice wavered into a thin croak. "Mind you," she tried again, "he wouldn't have heard anything where he was. I walked to the very end of those half-built houses I think, before I turned back. Tht boy was a long way back further towards town. But still . . ." She said sharply, "The houses! Of course! She ran into those houses and never came out again!"

"Looking for help? If she'd been there when you happened along she would have dashed out and grabbed you. Well?"

"You're right, so that means she didn't want help. She thought Carol was dead. She was . . . frightened of getting involved. There you are, Phil! It does add up. She was afraid of getting involved, saw or heard me and dodged into the houses. She thought to herself, 'Here's somebody else, thank God. She'll find the body and get help and I needn't so much as show my face'. There you are."

She looked at him triumphantly, but he said, "No."

"Why not?"

"Look at your own statement." He was rustling papers, looking down at the scrawled notes he'd made from questioning her before. "You say you left Larapinta and walked along the path to the end of those half-built houses. Then you noticed the angry sky. You changed your mind about visiting your old home . . ."

"Right. I was going to walk across the bridge to the old place and catch the subsidiary bus service over there home again. If I'd gone—she must have been in the water, Phil—she had to be—I'd have seen her long before Mrs. Buchanan saw that . . ."

He said wearily, "It's not a scrap of good, Gabriel. Go back to your statement. You turned back. You think it took you twenty minutes on the return journey."

"I expect so. I don't know for certain."

"The rain started as you hit town?"

"Yes."

"Place yourself by the end of the houses. That's twenty minutes before the rain started. About five minutes after that—only five minutes, remember—Mrs. Buchanan saw that woman. I went to see her. The two of us paced out how long it took her to get down to the creek. Ten minutes. Just that. She was bitter, speaking to me. She pointed out if the woman had only run on to the town, help would have been roused by the time the girl was being dragged out of the water. She says quite definitely that as she pulled Carol out the red sunset light went out. The place was almost in darkness and great drops of rain came down. A while later the storm proper started with a bang . . ."

"I remember that. The light was gone in a flash. It wasn't nearly time for the sun to go down, but suddenly every scrap of light vanished. It startled me and I stopped dead, almost blinded. Then I saw the bus pulling in and the crowd of women surging forward and I rushed to join them."

"You're certain of that. Mrs. Buchanan's certain of her facts too. She was as startled as yourself because she hadn't expected the storm to begin so quickly. She says she saw the woman, waited perhaps as long as five minutes, but she's sure not longer. Then she thought she'd just have time to satisfy her curiosity and take the dog for a run at the same time before the rain set in. She went straight to the hall, pulled down a coat and her stick and walked off briskly. Don't you see where that places you, if the story you're claiming is true? It turns you into the running woman yourself. You were there right at the moment . . ."

She said wildly, "It's all wrong. She was behind me. She had to be. She was behind me and she ran into those houses . . ."

"Why?"

"Because . . ." she stopped, fought desperately for an explanation and offered, "She couldn't have seen me in time to think I was going on to find Carol. I must have turned back by then, mustn't I? But look . . . no wait . . . yes, this is quite feasible. The woman sees Carol fall, or is responsible for it, and she tries to help, fails and so far as she knows the girl is drowned. She must have been hysterical, badly shocked, terrified. If she honestly thought the girl beyond help it's quite possible she ran into the

107

houses to compose herself a bit—she might even have thought she was going to collapse."

When he didn't speak she said shrilly, "it's quite feasible! Why do you have to try and find flaws . . ."

He broke in impatiently, "You heard no cries for help, from either Carol or the other person; no sounds of struggling in water; nothing at all? The wretched brat couldn't have sunk like a stone. There must have been five minutes or more while the girl struggled, the woman tried to help, while she waited, screaming for someone to come, till she thought the girl was beyond any aid at all. Five minutes? It'd be more like fifteen."

She shook her head, went back to saying, "It must have been over long before I came. Carol, I mean. The fall. She was . . . floating, you see . . . perhaps face up, just unconscious really . . . you can see that, can't you?" she was almost raging at him now. "Then the woman came along and saw her and ran away, shocked and frightened, thinking she was dead. And . . . she just didn't want to be involved."

"That doesn't ring true, and you know it doesn't. It's not impossible she'd think of what involvement in an unpleasant case would mean . . . when you've had time to think, when perhaps you'd run a long way and stopped for breath, you could think out the pros and cons of that; when your panic had died down a bit. But you wouldn't think of it in the flash of seeing a body floating in water.

"What would your own reaction have been? For a certainty you'd have yelled your head off in shock and horror, calling any help there was around. If you couldn't get her out, thought she was dead, you'd streak off for help—yelling for it to come. I simply can't imagine a woman not screaming, not dashing away frantically till she ran out of breath and had to stop."

He shook his head. "It comes back every time to one thing, Gabriel—you were the running woman. You have to be. You ran from the bridge, perhaps remembering Mark and expecting to get him to help. But . . . I wonder if you passing him disturbed his daydream by the water. He probably saw the sky then and tore off home as soon as you'd passed.

"So . . . what happened there on the bridge? I think you came face to face with Carol. I think she'd gone over and was coming back and the two of you met. You've said Mark recognised you from Iley pointing out your photo in the papers. I'm sure Carol did, too. She was the sort who'd press for details about you, think of meeting you and knowing you.

"So . . . she might even have half-passed you, knowing she knew your face, then remembered where and who you were and turned swiftly to cry, 'Mrs. Endicott!' ready to tell you who she was and . . .

"Gabriel," his voice was lighter, sharp with expectancy and eagerness, "is that it? Did she turn that way so swiftly that she caught her heels in the planks? Wrenched one free, but the other held and toppled her over? Is that it? Did you remember Mark and race back to try and find him to help . . ."

She went on shaking her head, slowly, endlessly. She knew the dragging silence was to give her time to think, to accept what he'd said, to say it was true.

She broke it by repeating, "I'm not the running woman," and they were left gazing at one another in hostility.

. . .

In mid-afternoon she went back to the front door, easing the venetian slats apart, gazing out as she'd gazed so many times during the day. With the passing of midday, with the stopping of the workaday world, the scene had altered slightly. The watchers who stared didn't stay so long; they were dressed for sport, or for an afternoon out. But the faces mirrored every face that had been there before, blank, watchful, waiting.

This time her gaze went first to the road, looking for Phil's car. He'd gone away after that silence, her denial, their awareness of anger and dislike towards one another. He'd said, "I'll leave you to think. I'll come back later. Don't go outside."

Neither of them had commented on the watchers at the fence. Now her gaze turned to them from the empty road. She saw white frocks, and thought of Monday with a cold revulsion for

109

the memory; saw tennis rackets and a little bent woman in a flowered hat; saw a newcomer arriving—an elderly man with a brown and white dog.

She watched him look closely at the house, gaze turning slowly to take in its width, its height, the land around it. Then his hands moved. Slowly, the action speaking of time in abundance to spare, he unfolded the little collapsible canvas stool he carried, placed it carefully in a patch of shade, settled himself, with the little dog at his feet, eased himself a little, settled more firmly, hands on knees.

She went on gazing in an anger that was close to sickness. How dare he, she raged silently behind the door. How dare he, the abominable old wretch, settle himself there as he might have settled himself at some sporting function, some outdoor show, waiting for entertainment?

She thought of the morning, of the police arriving; picturing the crowd pressing forward, a murmur rising, perhaps some bolder souls edging through the gate, running across the grass, peering into windows, trying to hear what was being said inside.

The police, she thought, and went running to the phone, dialling, waiting with impatience, then her voice was babbling, demanding that the police do something about the people outside.

Were they trespassing on her property, the answering voice wanted to know. They weren't. Then there wasn't any misbehaviour in their actions, was there?

She thought bitterly there was even mockery in the voice telling her the highway, the footpath was public property. She wondered if the police were actually glad the people were there; that they thought the watchful silent staring might make her crack, confess . . .

She said, "Surely there's some law about loitering. Surely I've read . . . surely you could send a policeman—to make them move on—make everyone keep moving instead of standing—I'm not a free entertainment . . ."

There was triumph in the small fact of making them do something for her, instead of against her. And the police car came quickly. She stood, peering through the slats, watching the crowd turn, staring at this new interest, till it turned, sped away again, leaving a young policeman there on the footpath.

She watched him speaking, and the slow movement as the watchers began to move. No one argued, but they didn't hurry either and the policeman made no move to chivvy them on. Confident his instructions would be obeyed eventually, he clasped his hands behind his back, turned, and stared . . . at the house.

When Phil finally came he demanded, "How long has *he* been here?" and she told him of her absurd little triumph.

He said, "Look outside now," and she went back to the door reluctantly. There were more people. Moving certainly, but slowly, pausing often.

Phil said, "You've been a fool. They wouldn't have sent a man on their own account, and have you accuse them of harrassing you. But you ordered him up. Don't you see what you've done now—giving rumour a further spurt! Everyone will say the police are keeping a close eye on *you*. You can," he told her brutally, "expect the main crowd tonight, when the theatres and the pubs have closed. You'll be the final touch to the night's entertainment . . ."

She said, without rancour, "Stop it. You're not going to make me crack by needling me. You, or the police either with their silly little policeman. Or that crowd, with their staring eyes . . ."

But later she wondered how long they could work through a haze of argument and accusation and conjecture and ideas that came to her in a flash, to be instantly exploded by Phil's swift counter-words.

She sat there, much later, letting his level voice flow over and around her, but hardly listening, because his arguments were so convincing she was even beginning to doubt her own mind and memory; to think that she could possibly be wrong; that somewhere on that Monday evening she had blanked out for a time through which Carol had died and she herself had run swiftly through that searing sunset.

And now it was nearly another sunset and another storm coming—she could feel it in the oppressive heat that seemed to be striking through the glass walls from the garden. Even the birds were quieted and silent under the stifling heat. She was sure that if she went outside there would be a black blank of cloud in the west as there had been on Monday and that in a little while, when the day began to die, the sky would look like red flames coming from a black cauldron of cloud. Someone had described the Monday's sunset that way. She vaguely wondered who it had been and pounced on the name . . . Miss Traill.

The woman had told Phil she had been riding back across the bridge in the sunset and . . .

But it's impossible, she thought.

She had been there in the red light riding towards the town. She had told Phil of noticing the black cauldron and red flames as she'd crossed the bridge. Or had she? She tried to remember . . . remembered only that the harsh red light hadn't begun till she herself, Gabriel, had turned back. And it had stopped when she'd reached the town. A bare twenty minutes. And Miss Traill, with her bicycle, had never caught up with her; had never seen Carol either; had never seen Lisa Buchanan; was seen herself by no one . . .

Speech babbled from her lips. "She must have been behind me," she cried out, holding out her hands in appeal. "Who says she had that bicycle? We've only her own word for it. She was behind me. She had to be. I can see it. I turned back. Behind me . . . came Carol. That's it! Oh please, Phil, try to see with *my* eyes. I've turned back. Carol's behind me. And behind her again comes Miss Traill. Not on that bicycle at all, but walking . . ."

"A regular procession in the sunset," he mocked

"What does that matter? It was the sunset that caused the procession, anyway. We were all hurrying home. Carol steps on to the bridge and behind her comes Miss Traill. Carol might have called to her for some reason. But Carol turned sharply, caught her heel, and over she went . . ."

She stopped, remembering Phil saying Miss Traill could swim. Truth, or a lie, she wondered.

She was still pondering that, trying to place Miss Traill in the position of helplessness, of shocked retreat to the shelter of the houses when Phil said flatly, "She wasn't behind you. She was well ahead of you. She must have been in the town before you so much as left it.

"Oh Gabriel, it's no good, I tell you!" There was blazing anger in his voice and eyes, but she found that easier to bear than the light mockery of voice allied to cold suspicion of glance. "Look, I went to see the confounded woman. I told her how Mrs. Buchanan and I had paced times out. I asked her to pinpoint herself, and she said, 'Thank heavens, I'm well out of it. I was home here just before the rain started. Just in time to save my washing. It was such a queer evening . . .' she went on talking of that. She spoke of the red sunset, but she wasn't on the path when she saw that. On the path she was looking at the sky, seeing black cloud and wondering if she had time to do her shopping before she finally went home. It was when she came out of one of the shops that she first noticed that blazing red sky . . . she was ahead of you. So that's another theory fallen to earth and buried," he finished brutally.

"No!" She clung to the idea desperately, defiant in the face of his weary head-shaking. "It has to be that way. Well . . . not exactly that. Look at this . . . there mightn't have been much noise. How can we *know*? Carol might have been too shocked to scream when she fell, and afterwards . . . she could have had her mouth full of water . . . I know that's beastly, but it's only too possible. And the woman . . . well, leave Miss Traill out of it—place some one else there—behind Carol, seeing her fall. She'd rush forward and . . . she wouldn't scream, Phil. Not at first. Carol would be in the water, bobbing up and down, spluttering and the woman would be saying things like, 'Try to shift closer to the bridge, so I can reach you . . .' Why, at first neither of them would panic. Would they? Carol would know there was help. The woman might think it would be easy to save her.

"Only it wasn't. So she didn't scream. She didn't think of it . . ."

She fell silent, trying to place a figure there on the bridge, kneeling, speaking to the girl in the water, trying to reach her, watching her sink.

A woman . . . which one . . .

After a moment she said, "Mrs. Brown," and went on picturing the scene with the woman hurrying across the bridge with her errand done, hurrying against the storm like all of the others. She'd seen Carol ahead of her and what more natural than to call her name, sharply, angrily, prepared to tell her off for her earlier refusal to help with the toys when the girl had been actually coming that way that day.

She put the idea to Phil, asking fretfully, "But why simply run away? That's wrong." He didn't answer and she was forced to go on puzzling at the question, till she cried triumphantly, "But it's obvious when you think of the relationship between the two! Carol didn't like Mrs. Brown. Mrs. Brown didn't like Carol. When the girl fell Mrs. Brown was *glad*. Oh, of course she didn't want the girl to drown—that's ridiculous, but she might well have started to laugh, to call down in petty spite, 'That jolly well serves you right you little beast!' And . . . Les Brown himself said Carol needed a good wash. Can't you imagine Mrs. Brown adding, 'It'll give you a good wash, too, and you need one, you little grub!' And then . . . Oh Phil, she can't have known the girl couldn't swim, or else she'd forgotten. Probably she thought the water's depth was less than it was; maybe Carol was even quite close to the bank or the edge of the bridge and she thought the girl could easily get out. If Carol had spluttered for help . . . and yes, that's infinitely plausible, too—Mrs. Brown might well have jeered, 'No fear! You get out yourself. I'm not coming after you to have you duck me under and half-choke me, you little horror!' "

She realised that he simply wasn't listening. She said sharply, "Phil! Listen to me . . ."

"I'm tired of listening to you," he said evenly. "I went to the Browns, too. Brown is furious over the way his wife's name has been linked with the woman. He told me . . . he'd like to screw your neck. Sherida Brown went over the bridge all right, but she went over very early. Not only to deliver the toys, but to visit a sister . . .

"A sister—if she thinks that's an alibi . . ."

"I grant you a sister might lie for a sister, but will strangers? There were two other people there. All three of them waited till Sherida Brown's brother-in-law came home. They were all there when the rain began and he drove them home, not even going near the creek because the car ford was out of action with the water that high. Well?"

She said wildly, "Then there was someone else. Someone who called . . ."

"No, Gabriel, it was you who called . . ."

"It wasn't. Please . . . look . . ." she said abruptly, "Perhaps Lisa Buchanan's lying. There wasn't a woman at all. She made it up. To . . . to . . . she pushed Carol . . . and then . . . she made it up to get herself out . . ."

She knew it was ridiculous, before he exploded the suggestion with, "She's the last person to need to lie. She had only to say 'I saw her fall and dragged her out'. Why see *you*, Gabriel, and try to involve you, because you have to be the woman in white.

"You asked me to picture things. I can. You asked me to picture a woman leaning over, looking down at a girl spluttering in the water. You've asked me to imagine her crying, 'Serve you right, you horrid little wretch!' and leaving her.

"Did it happen that way—to Carol—and to you?"

"No." She kept on repeating the word, over and over again, into the storm-laden heat of the disordered room.

. . .

She said abruptly, "Mark . . . Mark Zamia. Is *he* lying? What was he doing down there at the creek anyway? Carol was there, he was there. Why, of course they went down together! Brothers and sisters squabble," her voice was babbling again, "what if *he* hit and she fell and . . ."

"And he left her to drown? If you could get anyone to believe that, Gabriel, you'd perform a miracle." His face expressed the distaste, the disgust he felt for the suggestion.

115

"Yes, I know—it's mad. I'm sorry. I'm grasping at straws," she tried to smile. "Well think of this—they go together and . . . they part. Carol goes on ahead . . . and look, it's what I said before. She must have been ahead of me. Mark would know what time she went down. She went over that bridge and was coming back, *behind* me, Phil, when she fell. Mark had already turned back for home, before I turned myself. Neither of us heard anything.

"That fits in. It *has* to be someone who was behind Mark, behind myself, behind Carol . . ."

"We're back to the same alternative—or someone who was walking towards Carol, so they met face to face on the bridge. And you were the only one walking towards the bridge."

She shook her head. "Someone behind her," she said stubbornly. "I'll grant you it couldn't be Miss Traill. Or what's-her-name Brown. But how many other women are there in this district?"

He shook his head. "How many young ones with fair hair, who were by the creek, dressed in white? Who couldn't swim? Who later paid for silence about their being there . . ?"

She said furiously, "You'd have paid yourself! If you'd been face to face with that horrible pair, threatening you . . . making you imagine what it would be like trying to live and work in a place where gossip and whispers followed you all the time! I was . . . terrified, I suppose. And I never dreamt it would go on and on . . . I kept thinking, 'I'll find her soon . . . and I'll crow over the Zamias . . . I'll get my revenge . . .' oh I know, it sounds ridiculous now, but . . ."

"Why didn't you simply come and ask me to help you?"

"Because . . ." she stopped. Then she said evenly, "I was afraid of exactly this, of not having you believe me, I suppose. All right, I admit that, but nothing else. Discount the fact I was fool enough to pay the Zamias. How many other women are there . . ."

"I know only one. All right, all *right*!" He drew away from her outflung arm. His mouth twisted in mockery. "Is that what you did to Carol, Gabriel? Hit out at her in temper and panic . . .

116

wanting to hurt her as you'd been hurt by what she said to you?"

He shrugged, "But, all right. I'll go on asking questions. Where, and what, I don't really know, but I'll go on trying, but I'm afraid, Gabriel. Really afraid. Scared solid that every question I ask will only drag you a bit further into trouble."

CHAPTER TWELVE

His spine had become mutely resigned to the hard discomfort of the overstuffed chair, but neither eye nor nose had joined the resignation. The room's smell was compounded of many things—dust, stale cigarette smoke, stale humanity, cheap varnish and over it all the aggressive, overpowering reek of scented furniture polish. He wished, lighting another cigarette, offering one to the woman's greedily-reaching fingers, that they'd taken him into the kitchen. At least there there would have been Fred's sagging rocker to sit in and the smell of cooking above everything else, but even in the kitchen, he reflected in sharp distaste, he wouldn't be rid of the three of them.

There was a sharp revulsion in him at having any kindred at all with them; at being part of a humanity that included Fred's flabby body and stubby fingers picking at an inflamed pimple on his flattened nose; at sharing a past with the woman with her pathetically distorted body, her greedy eyes and restless mouth, the inflamed bunions showing through the cheap thong sandals; at sharing a name with the sullen, dull-looking youngster whose grubby fingernails were bitten to the quick, yet still being tortured by the eager teeth working on them now.

Mark Phillip Zamia, he thought wryly. Mark *Phillip* indeed, and damn Iley for the cheap sentiment that hadn't touched her eyes, only the oiliness of her voice saying, "A'course you were always my favourite, Phil. When we got to thinking of names I said to Fred 'One for a saint Fred, which won't do him any harm and might do some good and I was gone on young Phil Sturt long a'fore you came round, Fred, so what about Phil?' . . ."

He'd laughed at the time, believing none of it, but being tickled just the same and he'd come across with a handsome christening present, which was what she'd been angling for all along, he'd known.

Take what you can get and don't be backward in asking for it, that was Iley's creed, had always been so, and still was.

He went on sitting there, while his mind urged him to go, told him he was being a fool, that he could sit there till doomsday and the woman's eyes would hold no shame, and her tongue would twist the truth to please herself. And that in none of it was there help for Gabriel.

She was saying, "You know I'd do anything for you, Phil. We'll none of us tell that she was there by the creek, but I don't think it'll help you none, will it? Not from what I've heard round town.

"But what she's told you about us—that's lies. To save herself, I guess. Making out she *had* to pay us money. That's wrong. She offered it. Mind you, I'm not denying we told her Mark'd seen her. I was warning her, like, see. Telling her that what Mark'd seen other people might've too—telling her she ought to go to the police and make a clean breast a'things before a lot of dirty talk started. I haven't lived this long without finding out what dirty tongues a lot of folks've got. Mind you, me and Fred don't blame you for swallowing it, considering the old days and you two being so close, but those days're over. There's a long gap 'tween kids and folks the age of you and Gabriel now—a grown woman doesn't confide in a man like a bit of a girl with a boy "

True enough, but it was still impossible for him to change the known Gabriel of childhood with her passionate defence of friends; passionate protection for the unjustly accused; with her almost aggressive owning-up to scrapes to protect him and other playmates; with the woman who would grimly see anyone pilloried by gossip.

What on earth had the wretched pitiful girl said to her on the bridge? It had to be that, he was certain. Something said that frightened her terribly; made her roam the district asking questions about that night. Had it been about himself? It was horrible to feel part of it; to know that mention of his own name had caused it all. But more likely it had been about Nicholas, he thought wearily. Far more likely.

A picture jumped into mind—a wildly disordered house, an

exhausted slim body huddled against cushions. He was suddenly cold in the stuffy heat of the room. Was she heading for a disastrous breakdown, he wondered? There'd been that impossible job for her, constant fretting over this patient and that; her meeting with Nicholas and her rushed marriage . . .

And Nicholas, with his stress on perfection in anything around him, had been totally wrong for her. How long had it been before Gabriel had started worrying over her marriage? Because she had been. He was sure of that.

And then, Carol's death . . . and the knowledge she was responsible. No wonder Gabriel was acting oddly now. The girl's death must have been the last straw . . .

But what had the wretched little creature said to her there on the bridge?

It was difficult to remember, till Iley's voice jerked him from abstraction, that he'd come to question Mark in the forlorn hope that the boy might have seen Gabriel go back to the town; might have seen his sister after that, or heard something.

Mark's mother, he realised, was repeating what she'd already said over and over. "I'm not saying Fred and me didn't talk all round it and get in touch with her, and why not? Didn't we have a *right*, Phil? There was Mark'd seen her and she was in white, too and I remembered about her not swimming and that, and I had to *know*—well didn't I have a right to know what'd happened? I wasn't going to blow up at her; not anything like that. I just had to know how it happened. Fred'n me rang and see, she came, right off her own bat and sat there, right where you are," she pointed dramatically at the chair with a nicotine-stained finger. "She was all shaky like and she denied she was the woman true enough, but I could see she was scared silly. I'd have dropped it because we weren't doing anything good—she wasn't going to tell us anything. And then she gave me that cheque. Pushed it in my face. Isn't that so, Fred?" she appealed. "Told me to please spend it on a new pram or something. We guessed she'd seen the old one in the hall and I'm not denying it looks like junk. I was too surprised to say a word. And then after, we got a note from her—a messenger brought it. It said baldly that the funeral expenses for our Carol had been paid. Just that. Not a word more. We were staggered. I said to Fred, It's her conscience. A'course," she looked down at her hands, "now it's you who claims you paid them."

He stood up, feeling a sick gall rising in his throat, wondering why on earth he'd bothered with the family at all through the years, cursing himself for that gesture of paying for the funeral.

He turned away, crushing out his cigarette in a garish ashtray. He said thickly, "I'll be on my way." He added, "I'll see myself out," but all three of them crowded out after him so that the hall was suddenly a press of bodies against the tired paint on the walls and the battered cane perambulator.

In the confused moment he was aware of a hand in his, and revulsion, a sick horror and distaste, drew him sharply away, gazing into the upturned, sullen eyes of the boy. He jerked his hand roughly away; half-expected to hear the boy say something; see his expression change. There was nothing.

He went down the path at a lope, thinking that his namesake appeared half-witted. It wasn't till two streets away that he abruptly stopped the car again, to reach in his pocket for cigarettes, and felt the paper.

The mere sticky touch of it reminded him of the small hand. He drew the carefully folded square of exercise-book paper out and sat there staring at it. The queer moment in the hall was explained, and for a moment wild amusement at the memory of his revulsion, made his shoulders shake.

The reason for the boy trying to slip a note into his hand and finally into his pocket wasn't apparent at first, but the words of the surprisingly well-lettered note seemed to leap out and hit at him.

"There was another woman down at the creek. I didn't go home right off. I followed your cousin down to the houses. She never looked back once or she would of seen me. I nicked into the first of the houses. The workmen had gone away for the day. I was in the houses when it rained and after all the people came. When I knew about Carrie I ran home then. I didn't see the other woman come to the houses, but she was in the one nearest the bridge when I looked in there after a bit. I heard her crying and I saw her when she left. I didn't tell mum and dad because she wasn't in white. She had on a raincoat with big checks on it. Later on I saw her with the people round Carrie. She was crying again. If you want to know who she was you can ask me."

He re-read the note three times before he said aloud, mockingly, "oh no, Mark. No, indeed. I'm not paying for information. You're Iley's child all right, blast you."

And did it matter? He pondered that, and decided it didn't. Obviously Mark didn't think so either, or he'd have told long ago.

What did it add up to? Simply a woman, who wasn't in white, or Mark would have said so. And she hadn't seen the woman in white, or Mark, or Gabriel or anybody else, or she'd have come forward herself long ago. That simply left some unhappy soul who'd used the half-built houses as a secluded spot for a good weep. Later on she'd left the houses, drawn by the commotion, as Mark had been. Or she might have left before that. But in any case she had wept again, for the dead girl. Probably other women in the crowd had wept too. Lisa Buchanan for one . . . was she the weeping type?

And she probably knew the name of the woman in the raincoat, he reflected. It would make an excuse to go and see her again, to probe a little more, to try, even now, to help Gabriel.

But as he drove away towards the ridge the memory was clear again in mind of a wildly-disordered house and a glittering-eyed woman crying, "I hate it. You didn't realise that, did you? But I hate the house . . ."

There was another memory, too, of shaking eyes, of anxious eyes, of a wild voice accusing, "She was skiting she knew some wonderful secret about Bernice Strang . . ."

What the devil had the wretched girl said to Gabriel?

. . .

She was too tired to try and fix the house into some semblance of order. Only a tiny corner of thought reminded that it must be done before tomorrow—before the police came. All too easily she

122

could picture them moving round the place, as Phil had done, to come, glance at each other, at her, speculating, wondering about her whole life.

Ghost-like, in the dimness from the shuttered windows, she flitted from room to room; made coffee and left it undrunk on the sink; switched on the television set and then left it because there was no programme that didn't dwell on sport or pop music; turned on the radiogram to full pitch to drown thought with music, then left it too because the doorbell was ringing.

Only when she stood in the hall did she stop. She had thought at first, Phil, and had gone swiftly, because there was a flaming spark of hope that he had news; help for her.

Only standing still did she remember how little time he'd been gone; and start to wonder.

She went slowly towards the door, eased the slats slightly apart, looked out. The policeman was still standing near the fence, staring towards the house. There were one or two people the other side of the street, staring her way, too, and a cluster of children round the gate itself. There were one or two other people . . . and no one outside the front door.

Impossible, she thought, and wondered if she'd dreamt the sound, then her gaze went down and there was a child on the step, a boy in baggy shorts and bare feet, who couldn't be more than five at the very most, whose towhead was so short a distance from the ground she hadn't seen him at first.

She felt a smile tug at her mouth; the first in days. No need for panic here, she reflected. No reporter, no inquisitive neighbour, no policeman . . . just a small boy in baggy shorts and bare feet who was probably selling raffle tickets for some school project or other.

Or . . . with a message from Phil?

She didn't stop to wonder how absurd the idea was. She opened the door and promptly he took a step over the threshold, into the hall, facing her, grinning up at her.

She smiled faintly, asked, "Well?"

He chanted rapidly, in a sing-song treble, "We all know that Carol's dead, 'cause waters closed above her head, but Mrs. E.

123

please tell us all, was she pushed or did she fall?" A spluttering explosive giggle burst from his lips, and was silenced.

By the look on my face, she thought afterwards. How did I look anyway? If my face mirrored all I thought he must have been scared out of his wits.

It was instinctive to hide the panic, the sick shock, to seek oblivion from the staring faces beyond the fence. Her hand thrust out, shoving at him, so she could close the door, while anger, the thought of the words she would say to the police over the man at the gate letting the wretched, horrible brat come to the house, was her only thought.

She had no intention of hurting him, or even knocking him off his feet, but he went stumblingly backwards, tripped over the step, and crashed flat on his back beyond the step. She heard a sharp cry from somewhere beyond the gate, drowned instantly by the blubbering uproar from the child, then the heavy front door slammed shut and she was leaning against it, shivering in panic.

She could imagine the faces, hear the voices whispering. "The second time . . . once on the bridge . . . once here . . . just as well the poor brat wasn't near the river this time . . ."

Softly she moved backwards, into the front bedroom where she could still see the fence, the gate, the doorstep. She could see the gate opening and the policeman, absurdly young . . . didn't the district possess any older policeman, she wondered vaguely . . . coming slowly up the path, kneeling over the boy, urging him, still yelling, to his feet, ushering him towards the gate.

He stood there watching till the boy had gone beyond it, to become part of the group of children . . . the ones who'd put him up to that horrible chant, she thought bitterly. He'd been a mere baby—too small to have thought it up by himself.

Then the policeman turned, came up to the step. The doorbell rang. Twice. Then footsteps came slowly round the side of the house. She heard him knocking. On windows. On the back door. Softly, inside the shuttered house, she followed his knocks from room to room, back to the front again, watching him go down the path. He closed the gate carefully behind him, and spoke to the people clustered outside. They began to move. Quite quickly this time.

So now, when it was too late, she thought bitterly, he was standing no nonsense, though surely, fairness reminded her, it was hardly his fault he hadn't seen trouble in the guise of a five-year-old. The boy could have said he was a neighbour's child with a message, anything at all.

With the crowd gone, the policeman turned again, stared at the house and then began to move, quite briskly, along the roadway.

For a moment sheer terror nearly sent her flying to the door, the path, crying to him not to leave her alone, for fear a bigger crowd returned, perhaps with the child's parents, roaming round the house, battering on the door, demanding she open to them, to explain, if she could.

Then she realised he was simply striding towards the call box at the end of the road.

She thought, in sweet gratitude, He'll get someone else. Someone older. Someone to help him cope in case the parents *do* come.

Then relief was gone and she was asking herself if he was going to phone a report, and if, soon, a police car would come swiftly along and they'd ask her . . . what did they say in cases like this? Ask her politely to come to the station with them? Simply say they were arresting her?

They couldn't, she denied the whole thought aloud.

But they will, reason told her. They'll come and they'll question and they'll take down my answers and talk about it being for my own good that I'm not left here alone—in case of trouble in the night. They'll take me away.

What had Phil said about her playing into their hands by asking for the policeman? She had, and played into them again now by hitting the child and letting the man see.

She thought, I've got to get away. Quickly. Before he comes back.

.   .   .

He threw at her without greeting, "Who was the woman in the checked raincoat?"

125

He saw her small mouth gape. She had surprisingly big teeth and he found himself, for some ridiculous reason, fascinated by them, his mind quite blank, while he waited. Then her lips came together. She drew back, said, "Come in please," and led the way into the front room. She turned quickly to face him, went on standing, back to the window, gesturing him to a chair, then said, "What is all this?"

"I wanted to know if you saw a woman, Mrs. Buchanan. A woman in a checked raincoat. That Monday evening. Someone who was amongst the crowd at the creek, when help came. Someone who was there . . ." he hesitated, suggested, "There was a woman there, crying? Someone has mentioned seeing one."

She moved impatiently, her hands coming together in front of her for an instant, then thrusting outwards as though pushing the whole question away from her in impatience.

"Everyone wore raincoats. The storm had broken." The pupils of her eyes seemed to dilate with the memory. "The policeman had one of those huge absurd capes. No, there were two policemen. Another came after. It was the first one who removed his and put it round me. My teeth were chattering. Cold and shock together. I remember he said, so gently, 'You're getting soaked,' and I was too shocked to say the cape was useless. I was drenched to my skin, you understand? I had been in the creek water . . . I was so wet the rain could do no harm, yet I couldn't explain and he himself was getting drenched . . ." she gave herself a little shake. "But what is important about this woman?"

"She was crying . . ."

Again she thrust the question impatiently aside. "Women cry, at sorrow, at tragedy, at great joy . . . it is our safety valve. A woman couldn't bear the world otherwise. We are too emotional, too touched by everything that happens . . ." she shrugged, "I can remember someone saying over and over, 'Oh my God, oh my God', and one of the policemen—a boy really—he was swearing. That is a man's outlet—to swear. Ours is to cry. I cried myself perhaps—I do not even remember now." The pencilled brows went up in question. "Well?"

126

"You're right, of course. I just thought—this woman might have been about the first woman to come; might have helped her; might have shown more distress than others—I thought she might possibly have come along and you called to her for help . . ."

She stared, then shook her head. "No, no, you are quite wrong! There was no one. The storm was breaking, I tell you! The place was deserted. Just Carol and I. I had to leave her. I ran back here. I rang the police. I pounded on my neighbour's door, crying to her to come quickly, to bring others. I ran back."

"There was no one else here by then?"

"Of course not. I tell you, it was pouring with rain. There was only Bruno. I left him there with her. I made him lie across her for warmth, for protection from the rain." Her voice mocked bitterly at herself as she added, "I was like the policeman. Protect her from the rain, I thought, and she was already soaked from the creek. Shock makes one act absurdly. All I could think was, Bruno is warm, and big. He will warm her, stop the rain drenching her . . ."

Something tugged at thought. He looked at her, frowning, then said, "If the storm was beginning—didn't you think that woman in white was simply running to get home before she was drenched?"

"I have thought about that since." She moved across to the table, took a cigarette and lit it before going on, "but there was . . . I do not know how to explain . . . such a sense of great urgency in that flying figure. It wasn't mere hurrying. There was a tremendous haste . . . I can't explain, but I do know I did not even think of someone merely hurrying. I saw her and my mind said there was something very wrong. A woman would never run that way, using her whole strength and energy, against rain.

"That was why I left the house, even with the storm coming. I had thought before of taking Bruno out, but the sky was darkening. Then . . . well I went." Then abruptly she shot at him, "What do you think this other woman—in the raincoat—can tell you?"

"I thought . . . what if she'd come from those half-built houses? Been there inspecting them perhaps." At her frown, he hesitated, then decided against mentioning Mark. "Someone saw a woman there earlier—she was wearing a checked coat. I thought if she'd been there when Carol fell she might have seen the running woman go past . . ."

He stopped, his mind echoing the surprise in her startled, "That is absurd, surely? This woman must have gone for help. She must have cried out. If she was heard, seen . . ."

Of course, he thought in disgust. Mark hadn't been in the houses at all. The little wretch had been lying. He'd made up a story he'd thought might get him a few shillings reward—he'd have made up some vague description—but he couldn't have been in the houses or he'd have seen Gabriel, heard her when she came past the houses. She must have cried out, hoping some workmen were left there . . .

But *had* she cried out? If she had been responsible and thought the girl was dead, mightn't she have run silently away, trying to avoid being seen or heard?

Gabriel, he thought wretchedly.

Gabriel hearing something against Nick and himself, in connection with Berry Strang. Oh yes, it added up, all too plainly. Gabriel, hitting out, being responsible . . .

He stood up. Through the windows he could see the creek, and the trees that hid the bridge. There was a lowering bank of black cloud in the west, with the sky a brilliant searing red above it. The world had an unearthly rose-coloured light that he knew would end, in thirty minutes or so, as abruptly as it had begun. Later on, sometime in the evening or not, the storm would break in a grey, pouring deluge.

The scene outside now, he realised, must look very much as it had done on Monday when Carol had stepped on to the bridge . . .

He asked abruptly, "What do you think happened?" And when she didn't answer he said, "She was spiteful, I suppose you'd call it. Wouldn't you?"

She said crisply, "She was a very silly little girl. Oh yes, she was spiteful. If someone ignored her, annoyed her, she liked . . . to get even, as children say, and the only way a child her age of getting even was by her tongue, making up silly gossip. Why I

128

myself have heard her say things . . ." she broke off suddenly, her eyes blank.

A straight lead to Gabriel, he thought helplessly. Always back to Gabriel. Every question, every road, every idea, leading back to Gabriel being taunted in some way . . . about Nick almost certainly. But why? He frowned in suddenly upsurging doubt. There was something wrong about that. Carol was spiteful on occasion, but she'd never walk up to someone she didn't know, hadn't spoken to, had no grievance against, and say . . .

He went on frowning, forgetting the patiently-waiting woman at his side, only aware that there was something wrong; that for once the road didn't lead back to Gabriel. Gabriel and Carol hadn't met. That was a fact.

A fact? It wasn't, he realised in acute shock. It was merely what Gabriel had said.

But what if it was another lie?

Eileen Zamia had told Carol about Gabriel. Start with that, he told himself urgently. Start with Carol being interested, asking questions. And go on . . . to where?

To Carol going to the Endicott house, he thought grimly.

There was the reason for spitefulness. Back circled the road neatly to Gabriel again. Carol had gone to the Endicott house to introduce herself, try to make friends and worm herself into the place, thinking how she'd boast to her teenage friends about knowing the Endicott pair.

So Carol had gone to the house and Gabriel had turned her smartly away. It had to be that. Gabriel, seeing that unattractive child on her doorstep, might only have thought of Nick's disgust at having her inside his perfect house where she would have stuck out like a sore thumb.

So Gabriel had turned her away, pleasantly no doubt, but quite definitely. Carol, he had no doubt about it, would have been furious. She'd have wanted to get even; had possibly spent quite some time on plotting out how to do it, only to have any chance of it fading away because Gabriel had shut herself up in seclusion for months.

Probably Carol had forgotten the snub almost completely when finally the pair of them had met on the bridge, and then some imp of devilment had made her remember it, made her blurt out the secret she'd discovered, turn it into something nasty, unpalatable . . .

Gabriel had probably been open-mouthed in amazement, then shocked and finally angry. If the wretched girl had gone on standing there, blocking the way across the bridge, a push, an angry, "Get out of my way; let me past," was only too possible.

He decided he didn't want to think any more about it; didn't intend to speculate whether this thing or that had happened. In the morning, whether she liked it or not, Gabriel had to tell the version that would get her into least trouble—a story of Carol turning, recognising her, and catching her foot and falling . . . then an effort that was too much, and a collapse.

Outside he eased himself into the car behind the wheel, but sat there unmoving a moment, conscious that the woman was still standing on the step; as still as himself; that someone in a nearby house had a radio going too loudly, that a little dog, rosy pink in the storm glare, was coming darting up the street ahead of a small boy, and yet not really seeing any of it.

Only when his hand reached for cigarettes did he remember the note. He pulled it out, looking at it in disgust and then in sudden rage he tore it, shredding it to slivers and let them fall from the window into the still air, to snowflake the road.

Only when the last shred fell did he lift his gaze to the driving mirror. He could see Lisa Buchanan reflected in it and anger disappeared in impatience. She was staring, mouth slack, eyes wide. Something else for her to think about, he thought bitterly, driving away. He had probably looked half-crazy sitting there tearing violently at the small pieces of paper, scattering them.

Cloying weariness touched him again. He told himself it didn't matter. Nothing mattered. He was helpless. There was nothing to do except leave Gabriel alone for a night's reflection, and then let the whole wretched business take whatever course it could.

· · ·

Lisa Buchanan went on standing there long after the car had gone, gazing rigidly into space.

Why didn't I remember it?

The question was a dart of pain in a mind tortured by a flickering series of memories; a woman's sobs and a voice saying, "Oh my God" over and over; hands lifting herself, folding something round her and a gentle voice saying, "That'll keep the rain off"; Bruno's howls and her own voice saying, "Stay Bruno. Lie on her. Stay."; a woman running, running in desperation . . .

Why didn't I remember it?

She folded her arms round her thin body, hugging herself as though remembered cold was biting at her flesh.

What am I going to do?

The question was there as sharply as the first one, but this had an answer. She knew, as she turned abruptly on her heel and went back inside, slamming the pink door behind her, shutting out the world, that she wasn't going to do anything. Perhaps someone else would remember. Let them, she thought. Perhaps, finally, she might have to speak. Perhaps not. Whichever way it turned out, for the time being she was doing nothing. Nothing but sit behind her shuttered door, away from the world, away from questions and let things take whatever course they willed.

CHAPTER THIRTEEN

"I would have been a fool."

She spoke the words aloud to the dim house. The birds heard her voice and called to her over the noise of the radiogram and the television set. She turned slowly, seeing their small, bright bodies fluttering behind the silvered mesh and said knowingly to them, "I would have played into their hands again. If I ran away they'd say I was really *her*, and I didn't dare stay to face any more questions."

The night would be the worst, Phil had warned her. People would drive and walk past them, moving on; keep them from sneaking through the gateway, pattering across the unformed front garden, tapping at the glass, knocking at the door . . .

The phone bell was a relief. It brought an end to thought that was bringing a return to panic, but when she lifted the receiver, heard the crisp voice, took in the words, panic was a solid, hard knot stifling her breath deep in her chest.

She said, "But you can't . . ." and the voice broke in and flowed on and on.

She took in only half the words . . . "Saturday evening . . . always kept busy . . . speedway races . . . teenagers looking for trouble . . . two stolen cars . . . a traffic accident . . ." then the voice finished decisively, "We can't spare a man to patrol the front of your premises, Mrs. Endicott. Our man has phoned in and reported very few people, and all of them quite orderly, with no signs of trouble . . ."

Nonesense, she thought. He's reported about that boy. That's why you're doing this. You're leaving me without any feeling of protection. You want me terrified into running to you and confessing.

Her tongue spluttered into confused speech, mentioning the child, telling them what the chanting words had been.

It was the final straw that the youthful voice took on the mildly-chiding note of a grown-up towards a child telling tales out of school on another. "Oh well, Mrs. Endicott, a tyke that age wouldn't know the meaning of what he was saying. We can hardly go and paddle his backside, can we? And you've no need to open your door, have you? In any case there's a storm coming, and that should keep people off the streets. If something frightens you or . . . if you'd like to have a chat with us about anything . . ." the words hung heavily on the hot air, "just call us."

She wondered, cutting him off, what the police were doing, either to help or condemn her. Nothing probably, she fretted. They wanted to save themselves trouble. They'd give her time to think, then take her statement and start from there to investigate.

Restlessly, anxiously, she went back to the front bedroom, easing the slats aside, gazing out, drawing a breath that was almost a cry because the street was empty still. She had expected a crowd of avid, eager faces watching and mouthing about the child she'd hit; expecting her to provide some other tasty entertainment for a dull Saturday evening.

Instead the roadway and footpath lay deserted under the odd searing-red light of the stormy sunset, reminding her vividly of Monday, of a ribbon of pathway under the same light, and her quick, startled glance upwards at the sky, seeing it, as Miss Traill had said, as red flames in a cauldron of black cloud; seeing the birds, a stream of quick silent movement overhead as they sought shelter, seeing . . .

She went running back to the phone, lifted it and dialled, thinking of what she would say to him, but there was no answer and she knew she couldn't bear to wait. She had to see the wretched creature, get the truth . . .

It wasn't till the front door was open that she realised how long she must have stood, groping in memory, by the window, because the street was no longer quiet and deserted. It seemed to her startled gaze as though the district's people marched from either end of the roadway to clasp her in their avid grasp, while they questioned and probed. Even when her gaze focused fully and she realised one group was the local riding club astride their ponies and that the other was mainly children, with the tow-headed five-year-old in their midst, panic remained.

She knew she could no more go outside and try to pass them than she could still the panic. Even in the car . . . she thought of trying to drive with the children, in mocking devilment, darting in front of her, riding their ponies at her, not letting her go more than a snail's pace, so they were able to jeer at her through the windows, chant at her, "Mrs. E. please tell us all, was she pushed or did she fall?"

Even if she waited . . . the thought was dismissed almost as soon as it came. It was impossible now the policeman was gone. He'd driven away the adults. Perhaps they were ashamed to come back; even pitying her behind their own closed doors. But children were different. Released from any supervision by adults, by the policeman, they'd stare and tease, laugh at the word trespass and come through the gate, tapping, calling, "Mrs. E. please tell us all, was she pushed or did she fall?"

Get away, thought urged. Out the back before they reach the house and screw up courage to come through the gate and round the place. Run out the back, through the new fence, double away into the scrubland and work round to the road again . . .

She remembered, in time, the fair hair that was going to draw sharp eyes to her wherever she went, grabbed a scarf and bundled herself into a mackintosh, then fled out the back door, a mingling of birdsong and the crooning of a pop singer giving a mocking farewell to her going.

Everything, as she ran, doubled in on herself so she wouldn't stand out sharply and be seen, reminded her of Monday—herself, a running figure through the red sunset; the birds, a long streamer of colour across the sky; the way she glanced upwards to stare at them and the coming storm . . .

She went sprawling, too shocked even to yell at the pain in her foot, the agony of her body striking with full force on something that stayed solid for a moment, then splintered and gave way beneath her.

Shock was still too great for outcry as her fingers scrabbled for

134

handhold and were drawn agonisingly over rough stonework as her body rolled and bumped and crashed downwards.

She didn't dare move. Not for a long time, till she was sure that she wasn't going to fall further, till she realised the vast red glow was the sky away above her, and that she was in one of the Wells By-Gosh.

Absurd, lying there bruised and shaken, to remember that absurd little story Phil had told her, of the disastrous drought twenty, thirty . . . she couldn't remember now how many years ago, but a man had come round the district claiming he was a water diviner. One of the farmers had had two wells put down, spending what was a small fortune for the time, and they'd both run dry in a month, with the diviner scratching his head and muttering over and over, "Well, by gosh, what d'you know?"

She concentrated on remembering the story, of Phil and Nick telling her the old farmland with the two wells was somewhere at the back of the Endicott house; both of them still dry, half-filled with rubbish and boarded over; while she eased herself upright to a sitting position and felt for damage.

She thought of later explaining to Phil that she must have come to the low stone coping round the top of it without even seeing it, because she'd been concentrating on keeping herself out of sight among the scrub, and had actually been looking at the sky, so that her foot must have slammed against the stone, throwing her smack on top of the rotten boarding over the top.

She could almost hear his laugh, see his mocking clown grin as he jeered, "Bumble-foot!" She could hear herself mocking back, "Well by gosh, and I came down with only a few cuts and bruises. Well by gosh, I really did . . ."

Shaky laughter bubbled to her lips and was gone. She looked at the red glow above her, and question probed, How will Phil, or anyone else, know I'm here?

CHAPTER FOURTEEN

Damn Mark, he thought bitterly, as he drove away. Damn him and his note and the senseless little lie.

No, not senseless.

He had slammed on the brakes so viciously that the car jolted, swerved and went into skid. For a heart-stopping moment he thought it was going to turn over, then it was still again. His hands were sweating when he started it moving again, off the crown of the road where it had finished up, parking it against the kerb, sitting there with a racing heart, getting himself under control again, thinking back to that minute of dismay when he'd realised the lie couldn't be dismissed as senseless because it was going to cause further trouble for Gabriel.

If Mark came out with that lie, and stuck to it, it was going to look to the world as though she had never tried to seek any help at all, but had simply fled from the creek.

Everyone would believe then that she'd struck the girl; not simply tried to help when Carol had turned too sharply and fallen.

Mark had to be made to say, now, that it was a lie that wasn't going to be repeated in public, he decided.

He sat on, mulling that over, searching for some ammunition to use against the boy, to confound him and force him into the truth. If he simply went now he had a good idea the boy would sullenly stick to it. And there was his mother, and Fred Zamia. They'd support the boy. By the time they were all finished that lie would have become solid truth and Gabriel would be completely damned.

So . . . what to do?

He went thinking over that Monday afternoon; over the people, picturing Gabriel leaving the bus; Carol leaving home; Miss Traill leaving her tennis party . . .

He thought suddenly, Where the devil was Mark when Miss Traill rode down the track? She didn't see him, but Gabriel did and the two women must have just missed one another in town by the look of things. So where had Mark suddenly appeared . . .

Mark, he thought. Mark and Carol. Going somewhere. Coming back together of course, across the bridge. Behind Miss Traill. And Mark arguing with his sister, giving her a good shove . . .

But he wouldn't have left her in the water. It was unbelievable to think that of a ten-year-old.

Irritably he poked at the problem, thought back in memory of days when he'd been Mark's age, crossing the bridge.

Of course! The answer was there, he realised. The two of them had been together, behind Miss Traill. And the girl's foot had been caught by the heel of her shoe. The boy had probably laughed and she'd said something on the lines of "Help me pull it free, beast!" and he'd laughed again, yelled, "Do it yourself!" and darted away, run so she wouldn't catch up with him when she was free again; run so hard he'd soon been out of earshot. And she'd stood there, still caught, yelling insults after him, then she'd tried to drag the heel free to get at him, toppled . . .

Good God, he thought in a cold shrinking disgust. That was it. The girl might have held on to the bridge for a little, tried to struggle back on and finally lost her hold. There'd been no one to hear her. And the boy had sat innocently on the creek bank further along, waiting for her to catch up so he could dart off again, taunting at her.

He must have begun wondering what was wrong by the time Gabriel arrived and he'd followed behind her. That was the truth. He might have thought the girl was waiting for him to come back, when she'd pounce on him and box his ears. He'd thought of Gabriel's presence as insurance against that happening.

Couldn't it have happened that way?

He went on probing at the idea, seeing Gabriel reach the water, seeing her find the girl floating, apparently dead, seeing her turning, shocked and frightened, crying out. And the boy? Of course, he'd been alarmed. Dodged into the houses out of sight.

He'd seen Gabriel go rushing back, and later he'd gone to the water, seen Carol, had been frightened out of his own wits, so that he'd fled home before Mrs. Buchanan had come.

But why hadn't Gabriel fetched help?

The thought went nagging desperately. And suddenly the solution was there in front of him.

The very thing he'd suggested himself had actually happened. She'd reached the town and felt faint; perhaps known she was going to be violently ill from a combination of shock and the desperate run. That's why she'd thought immediately of that excuse she'd given the police. She'd actually been in that public lavatory. Because of the storm, of people rushing for home, the place would have been deserted. She might have to stay there a long time, hoping someone would come. Finally she'd gone out, met hurrying men; seeing the ambulance perhaps. She might even have asked someone in the crowd by the bus stop what had happened and been told about the girl.

She'd known then she couldn't do anything. She must have felt only relief, a desperate need to get home.

He went on probing, seeing Gabriel, white-faced in the half-gloom of the lavatory, hearing steps coming in perhaps, shrinking away. But the newcomer might have paused, said, "Have you heard? They've found a girl in the creek . . ."

It could have happened that way. Easily.

But why had she lied? Kept on lying?

Why lie, when the truth would get her out of . . . but it wouldn't get her out of trouble now, he realised. Rumour had gone too far. She was afraid of that, now, of a manslaughter charge. Because there was no one to back her up.

Except Mark.

Mark, he thought viciously. Mark Phillip Zamia with his dulled eyes and his smooth lies!

He was already turning the car towards the Zamia house, then stopped. He needed some sort of proof before he tackled Mark and Iley and Fred. None of them were going to admit it if they could help it . . .

Miss Traill, he thought again. Ask her about Mark first.

. . .

138

She had managed to make out that the bottom was a jumble of loose stone. The sunset light didn't penetrate to the bottom of the narrow shaft, but her aching, grazed fingers had felt it easily enough and for a moment she had known stark panic, crying out with the force of it, wondering if the stone came from the circular walls and that at any minute the last of the stone might come breaking away, crashing down on her, burying her.

It wasn't till her groping hands told her the pieces were too small, too smooth, ever to have been part of the well lining that she worked out the rubble must have been placed there deliberately, in case of the sort of accident she'd had herself. In the beginning the well shaft had probably been much deeper, and anyone crashing in would have finished up with a broken neck. Before they'd boarded it over they'd filled it half way or more with rubble. Possibly in the beginning the rubble might even have filled it quite closely towards the top, only time and the undisturbed years had let the rubble settle slowly downwards.

She stood upright, slowly, hands pressed against the rough brick lining, gaze upraised and the red sky seemed so close she said with mocking confidence, to the rough brick under her hands, "Well my gosh I'll be away from you in next to no time."

There had to be a ladder of sorts, she was confident. There was a vague memory of something read about wells having to be inspected at intervals, and the usual thing was to insert iron rungs at intervals in the well lining. Rungs, or rings. She couldn't remember, but her grazed hands went groping round the brick, reaching above her, then she was kneeling close to the rubble and trying again.

Finally she had to admit that either her memory or the article she'd read was wrong, because the well lining was that and nothing more.

It didn't disturb her. It was simply an annoyance, because it meant she would have to find finger and toe holds in the lining itself and edge herself up that way. She'd felt cracks wide enough for that. She wondered, feeling for them again, if any of them were deliberate finger and toe holds left there instead of a ladder.

If there'd been more light she could have made sure and probably found a simple and quick exit.

Her glance upwards was impatient for the light not penetrating far enough down. It was even dimming, she fretted. Dimming, she realised in panic, even as she was looking at it.

The thought that she might have to spend the night there brought her, murmuring protest, back to the well lining, feeling over it, inching one foot into a space and reaching her right hand into another. It was both harder and easier than she'd imagined—harder because the cracks she was finding were far too shallow to be deliberate, but easier because they were so numerous she had little difficulty in hauling herself slowly up from one stretch to another.

She couldn't believe it when they petered out, but the light was so much better there close to the top that she could see the reason. Whoever had built the well had ceased the rough stonework below the coping and, probably for a pretty effect, she thought bitterly, had faced the last stretch with smooth, interlocking stone where there was no grip at all.

She was tantalisingly close to the broken planks, so close it seemed impossible her stretching hand couldn't even touch the edges of them. She held her position, fly-like, for as long as possible, but her hands were so sticky with sweat they finally wouldn't grip and she slipped and scrabbled back to the stone rubble and leaned back against the well wall, staring upwards.

"All right, then," her voice echoed gently round her, "keep me. We'll have to put up with each other until tomorrow."

The thought, she found, when looked at closely, wasn't so terrifying after all. Tomorrow was Sunday and a Sunday meant people —children playing, adults going slowly across vacant land, always with an eye to a likely building site.

Panic tried to return when she remembered the closed well top. If the place was a likely way for traffic, she reminded, it was astonishing the cover hadn't been broken in long ago by the curious. She fought the panic with the reminder the well had been right in a patch of scrub. She'd deliberately avoided a narrow, straggling scrap of path a short distance away. People who trod the path were unlikely to go raking around in scrub for the fun of it, but they certainly would if they heard a loud enough noise.

She tried the effect of a small piece of rubble tossed against the well wall and was childishly delighted at the echoing loudness of the simple action.

"All right," she told the well, "you're stuck with me, and I'm stuck with you. Till tomorrow. I'll hate the dark and the wet, because I'll be soaked when the storm . . ."

Panic was back. Great waves of it. She thought of Monday's storm that had gone on and on, deluging the world with rain. It had been the sort of evening she remembered from childhood, when the district's water supply had simply been tanks against the side of each home. On evenings and storms like Monday's the family would sigh with relief, and cry, "full tanks tomorrow", and listen with satisfaction to the gurgle of water running into the iron tanks.

She looked round the narrow shaft and thought, This is a tank, too. How will I manage? How long will it take to fill?

Her feet scrabbled against the rubble and were still. Was the rubble really a form of drainage, she wondered hopefully—an insurance against the well filling with so much water it would be unable to drain away somewhere underground for so long it became stagnant and a breeding ground for mosquitoes? She was sure suddenly that the rotting wood above couldn't have kept the place dry all the years of its abandonment. Probably quite a bit of water had come through with each period of rain, draining away slowly through the rubble.

But how long did it take to drain away? It couldn't possibly drain away like water down an open plug hole. There were probably days or even weeks . . .

Not that she minded. There'd been rain on Monday. Some must have filtered through the boards and the well was dry again now. But the place had been partly protected then, she remembered. Now it was fully open. It could be several weeks before a night's deluge would soak finally away.

141

More important still—vitally, terribly important now—was the question—how long would it take to fill? Before the water rose steadily upwards, over her head . . .

"We all know that Carol's dead, 'cause waters closed above her head . . ." came the chanting, mocking memory.

CHAPTER FIFTEEN

"*Mark* Zamia?" Miss Traill echoed. "Did I pass *Mark* Zamia on my way home?"

Irritated by her astonishment, he said, "Carol's brother. Ten years old. Rather like Carol. Sitting on the creek bank."

She shook her head, then demanded, "Do you mean he says he saw me? You mean . . ." she blinked, rubbed one hand slowly over her left knee, "he was with Carol?"

He asked again, "*Did* you see him? You surely couldn't have overlooked him on that path, could you?"

She seemed half-asleep he thought irritably. Only when he moved impatiently did she say at last, "I don't remember seeing a boy at all. Perhaps . . . he might have been in those houses. When I passed by. That sort of place is a terrible temptation to a child."

"I think he was there. Later. Miss Traill," he leaned forward, trying to wake her, with a louder voice, from her vagueness, "Try to be sure that Mark wasn't there on the path when you passed, because he might be responsible for this mess."

He began to speak, urgently, throwing the words into her blank, expressionless face. When he stopped she gave a little start, a little shake of her grey head. She said, "Oh no, you're wrong. You can't excuse her like that. It's not true. If it's right she never tried to get help. She can't have, you see. She can't have called, or knocked, or . . . I'd have heard her and you . . ." she stopped.

He began impatiently, "You haven't been listening to me. You were gone . . ." and then he saw her eyes. He said, "You've been lying!" almost in wonderment.

She shook her head. "How ridiculous!" Her body stiffened in the chair. She tossed her head. "How ridiculous. Of course I didn't lie. I was confused. You were speaking so rapidly. And you see, it happens . . . I paused on my way back, looking at those

143

houses. Such a temptation you know, to . . . to sticky-beak." She ventured a smile. "The workmen had gone. Really you know, it's disgraceful the hours they work. No supervision of course. They knock off whenever they please. This was quite early I suppose. I thought, why not have a look? So I stopped and . . . then when you spoke of the houses . . . it was confusion. I'd been there . . ."

He said grimly, "You're lying. Lying your head off Miss Traill, you told me you were wondering if you'd manage your shopping and get home before it rained. You were anxious about it. You were hurrying. Now you're trying to make out that in the middle of your hurrying and worrying you stopped to sticky-beak over houses you must have seen dozens of times before.

"Dear heaven, you sat there this morning," he raged at her, "babbling about your confounded washing, your sheets and your towels and everything else and how you just managed to get them in before the rain . . . washing!" he said explosively and grinned mirthlessly. He said quietly, "You liar! You were behind Gabriel, weren't you? Did you realise you wouldn't reach town before the rain began, and shelter in the houses? Or are you the running woman."

"Ridiculous," her lips mouthed, but no sound came.

"No. It's not ridiculous. You've lied. Why? Shall I ask round the neighbours, Miss Traill?" he raged at her, because now memory was strong, of his mother telling them all that someone down the street was ill, because sheets and pyjamas were out though it wasn't wash-day; of another day when she'd known of visitors next door because the fancy sheets were out. His father had roared with laughter, and his mother had tossed her head, admitting laughingly that the neighbourhood clothes-lines were eagerly watched by house-bound women. "Did you have to hang all your washing out again on Tuesday morning? Because you never came home till well after the rain started?" His voice pounded at her, "Did the neighbourhood women comment to their husbands over breakfast on Tuesday that you must have got caught in the storm because your washing was out again? They'll have noticed, Miss Traill. They'll soon call you a liar . . ."

144

She said, quite levelly, "All right, I lied. How clever of you to think the neighbours would soon prove it. I forgot about that. It was . . . I haven't anything to hide. You have to believe me!" Now her eyes were desperate again. "It was this gossip—it was horrible—and I was frightened. I'd been dressed in white, you see. I decided I'd prove I was home here before the rain began, when Mrs. Buchanan pulled that poor child out of the water. I thought —if I say I was well away from the creek at that time no one will talk about me any more. So I lied. I never dreamt it was going to lead to more trouble. You see, when it must have happened I was still there, at the creek. Oh not by the bridge!" She dismissed that impatiently. "I was in those houses. There are nine or ten of them. I didn't see that boy, but I did hear sounds. I thought I was dreaming it, or perhaps the workmen hadn't gone completely—that one had stayed on, and was out of sight from me. I didn't want to see him."

She sighed. "You see, I really was worrying about my washing. I came across the bridge—no, don't ask me when. I simply don't know. But the cloud was banking up in the west. And I had shopping to do before I got home. It was looking at the sky that brought me into trouble. I wasn't looking where I was going, and I'd hardly mounted the bike again before I must have hit a stone. I was thrown quite violently off."

Her hand dropped to her left knee. "When I struggled upright I saw the tyre was punctured too. But I'd hurt my hip and my knee. I was badly shaken too. I wheeled the bike to those houses actually I did mean to try and go on and then I felt terrible and my knee was bleeding. I wheeled the bike into one of the buildings and got out my little first aid case from the bike carrier. I fixed my knee, inspected my hip, repaired the punctured tyre on the bicycle. No, I don't know how long I was there," the impatience was back in her voice. "But I did notice the way the sky was turning a horrible red when I was in there.

"When I'd fixed everything I sat there for a little. I was badly shaken, as I told you before. There was a handy pile of wood, so I just sat."

Her lips quivered. "I didn't think lying would cause any trouble.

I did leave the tennis party quite early and that could be checked, and by the time I did leave the houses and go home there was such confusion . . ."

"You didn't leave till help came for Carol."

"That's right," she agreed wearily. "While I was sitting on the wood the rain began. I thought to myself, That's that. I might as well go on sitting there in the hope it would stop again.

"Actually," she looked down at her hands, "I heard the dog howling. I . . .I never paid any attention. I blame myself for that. But how was I to know?" she cried despairingly, and then she threw at him, "What I do know is that no one came to those houses crying and knocking for help. I couldn't have failed to hear it. I didn't see anyone pass, but I only looked out the window a couple of times. I didn't see the boy either, though I expect those sounds were him moving around. But I do know that no one came knocking and crying and seeking help."

And however way anyone looked at that, he thought despairingly, it condemned Gabriel. People couldn't fail now to say she had gone by silently, deliberately avoiding attention, because she'd struck the girl . . .

What on earth had the confounded little wretch said to her?

Because it simply wasn't possible she would have flashed by the houses if she'd simply seen the girl floating.

He said abstractedly, "So Mark didn't lie at least. You were the woman in the checked coat."

"What?" she jerked.

He told her of Mark hearing the woman weeping; seeing her leave; seeing her by the creek later.

She stared in astonishment. "It wasn't me then. I certainly didn't start crying over my injuries. My reaction was sheer rage! And I haven't a checked raincoat. I had a blue plastic cape in my carrier basket. I slipped that on before I left."

Another woman still, he thought in astonishment. Another woman who'd fallen, perhaps . . .

He looked at the woman opposite with critical eyes, doubting eyes. He said quietly, "Can you prove your story? Any word of

146

it?" His gaze fell to the hand still pressing on her left knee, "Except that you injured your knee? Did you do it that way? Or on the bridge?" He threw the words now at her gaping mouth, her rounded eyes. "Did you get into some argument with that wretched girl and hit at her? With your tennis racket perhaps? Did she clutch at you perhaps and bring you crashing down on your knee on the planks? Did you run away then, forgetting the bike, not realising she couldn't swim—just wanting to recover your composure? That could have been when Mrs. Buchanan saw you. And then, while she was getting her coat, starting off, you could have gone back, thought the girl had got out and gone because you couldn't see her, collected the bike and found the tyre was flat, so that you dodged into the houses . . . you never caught up with Gabriel. And you never went for help because you thought the girl had scrambled out.

"Aren't I right?" He thrust at her.

As quickly as the angry desperation had forced him into speech it died away. He felt a disgust, a sick gall rising in his throat as he looked into her ravaged, panic-stricken face.

He said, almost gently, "Am I right? Did you . . ."

"Oh no, oh no," the sound was barely a moan of denial. "It's not true. And . . . there was this other woman," she spoke quickly, in appeal. "The woman in the raincoat. Who is she? Perhaps she saw me and can tell what I did. Who is she?"

"I think Mark Zamia knows. I'll have to ask him." He was suddenly, wearily, convinced that the spinster was telling the truth. And that left Gabriel as the running woman . . .

Or did it?

See Mark, he thought wearily. See him away from Fred and Iley so they couldn't put words into the boy's mouth.

He went away thinking of that. With the storm coming the boy would be home now of course, so . . . ring him up and ask him to come somewhere? He could picture the result—a conference with the parents wondering suspiciously wny the boy was wanted. It was a certainty one or the other would come with him; that they'd warn him beforehand not to answer any questions at all.

Tomorrow, he thought in satisfaction. It would have to wait till the morning. The boy had a Sunday morning paper round. Easy enough to lie in wait for him and offer to drive him on his rounds. The boy would accept that and afterwards there'd be time and privacy for a long talk.

And for tonight?

It was pointless telling Gabriel of Miss Traill's lies. Lies or truth the woman was no help at all.

He went on hesitating, then turned the car. He'd pass the Endicott house. That for a start. If there was a crowd, he'd go in and perhaps stay the night, but didn't think there'd be trouble. The storm was a blessing, he reflected. Everyone would stay indoors and she'd be free from gawpers once the rain began.

So he'd simply pass by and make sure all was well.

. ˄ .

She wondered, pressed against the well wall, gazing up at the still red sky, if Phil would come back to the house. There was hope in that idea, because he'd had the keys to the place ever since Nick's death. He wouldn't be turned away by the doors remaining closed. He'd go in and find her gone.

She knew he'd jump to the conclusion she'd run away.

Even if he didn't, even if he didn't simply lock up the house and go helplessly back to his own flat, it wouldn't be any good. He might stay for a long while, waiting for her to come back, but in the end he'd be as wise as when he first found her gone.

He wasn't instantly going to beat his brow and cry, "She's fallen down a well!"

The thought made her laugh and relaxed her, but when she looked upwards the laughter died again. She had to do something, but she wasn't sure what. Her feet scrabbled restlessly, and stopped.

She thought, almost vaguely, If I manage to build some of that rubble into a sort of series of steps against the wall I'll be lifted higher and higher. Out of the water if the shaft fills. And closer to the top, too.

I might, she thought, and a helpless giggle rose in her throat, build myself a neat little staircase to the sky.

. . .

Miss Traill stood by the front windows, her hand holding the curtains aside, till the car was out of sight, and surprisingly, the one thing she could think of was that her knee was aching abominably.

How crazy to think of it . . . now . . . she reflected, letting the curtain fall back into place. How absurd to concentrate on an aching knee when everything was crashing about her ears. Phillip Sturt was going to create trouble. He'd hurt anyone at all so long as Gabriel Endicott was out of trouble.

"Prove it," he'd told her. The words taunted, reminding her she couldn't. That deserted creek pathway was there in front of memory . . . and she herself, rising painfully from the ground beside the bridge, looking up at the sky, saying two sharp short explosive words as she thought of the washing waiting at home . . .

She made a little sound of annoyance, remembering the lace curtains she'd taken down and washed before starting on another spell of painting in the spare bedroom. She went slowly to the back of the house, still conscious only of her leg, but then she stopped, the coming storm forgotten, remembering.

She was plunged back to another evening like this one, with a black cauldron of cloud and the searing red of all the sky above it. For a minute she didn't see the long narrow suburban garden beyond the windows, but a stretch of muddy water, an old plank bridge, trees whose branches were unmoving in the storm-pregnant air, houses sharp-etched beyond, in front of her.

Why didn't I remember?

She could feel her body trembling with the shock of memory, the wild exhilaration of discovery.

She said aloud, still standing there, "It couldn't be." And thought, I must talk to someone. I have to tell someone, to discuss this, talk it over, decide . . .

She thought again, Gabriel Endicott! I must talk to her first.

She was there, too and she *must*, surely, have seen that . . .

There was no pain in her leg now. She ran, unencumbered, to the phone, to the directory, her hands flicking at the pages, finding a number, dialling.

. . .

His first thought was the question about the policeman. There was no sight of the youngster outside the fence. No one else stood staring, either, and while there was relief in that, he wondered where the policeman was; wondered in sharp surprise if thought of the coming storm had driven away both the starers and the police.

Or . . . had Gabriel called him inside and made a statement?

He was out of the car, running up the path, leaving the gate swinging violently behind him, and almost crashed into the woman coming round the side of the house.

She gave a little shriek, darting back. She began, with the flushed anger of shock, "Why don't you look . . ." then said, "Mr. Sturt!" in something close to relief.

He recognised the sturdy, pink-clad figure as Gabriel's nearest neighbour, who had tried, like himself to winkle Gabriel out of her nun-like shell, only to be rebuffed by an impatient indifference.

Now she stood pointing to the house, saying, "Listen to that!"

In spite of the shuttered windows the sound of the blaring radio was quite distinct. She pressed, "If you ask me she's sitting in there scared stiff. I've been trying to make her open up and come on home with me for the evening. George and I wouldn't worry her."

No, he thought cynically. You'd just question her, try to get the truth out of her, and then was sorry for the cynicism, because her round face was creased with genuine worry and she went on, "I know what's being said. The people in the pub say she was by the creek Monday, dressed in white. Is that true?"

"She was in Larapinta," he admitted.

"But she wasn't by the creek?" she pressed and when he didn't answer she shrugged, "all right, it's none of my business I suppose,

150

and it'll all come out in the wash of . . . the inquest, hmm? However it was, anyway, you couldn't convince me it was deliberate, but . . . she's been odd, hasn't she? And," she jerked her head towards the house again, "you listen to that. I'm frightened for her. It's a pity it's the weekend and the kids are free of school. Some of them came round and started in teasing her, and then running round the house, calling out . . .

"There was a policeman a bit back. I saw him myself. Goodness knows where he is now, because I can't find him. But a teenager on a pony came up to our place and asked George if he could come and chase the kids out."

She sighed. "She was nearly in tears. Supposed to be in charge of the pony riders, she told us, and they wouldn't listen to her. They'd taken a lead from some boys—real bad lots from what I can make out. George went down with his brother and made a row." She bit her lip, then told him how the men had got hold of the story of the child's chanting and Gabriel hitting at the boy.

She finished, "George and Hartley chased the lot of them out and I've been trying ever since . . . I'm frightened for her, sitting cooped up in there all alone."

He tried not to let his anger, his sickened dismay and fury against the children, show in his voice and face, reminding himself it was hardly possible to blame children for acting badly when they'd probably heard all their elders speculating and even condemning Gabriel.

He said evenly, "She'll be all right, Mrs. Frame. I have the key and either I'll stay the night or I'll bring her up to you. Later on. When I've talked to her."

He didn't dream that she wouldn't be there to talk to at all. The birds called to him pettishly as he moved round the house from room to room, turning off the television and blaring radiogram; noting the uncleared mess in the kitchen; switching off the lights.

He noted, despairingly, that her mackintosh was gone, and also the scarf she usually wore with it. It was impossible to kid himself that she'd merely slipped out for a breath of air. She wouldn't have dared show her nose outdoors after experiencing the chanting children.

Where had she gone? He fretted at that, thinking of the crowded city where she might lose herself for a long time, of a lonely motel room, of a long car drive . . .

But the car was still in the garage. He went through from the door between it and the house, then returned, puzzled, because the car was surely the thing she'd have thought of for a getaway.

She hadn't meant to go far he thought suddenly and was immediately seeing his own flat, and Gabriel crouched on the dark landing, waiting for him to come back, seeking shelter and comfort for the night.

As he made for the front door again the phone rang, but he didn't bother with it. A phone call wasn't important. Getting to Gabriel was.

CHAPTER SIXTEEN

Gabriel leaned back against the well wall. She had removed the mackintosh because the exertion had made her unbearably hot, and now she could feel sweat trickling down the insides of her arms, and down her back.

She knew, if there'd been light enough to see, that her fingers must appear scraped and bleeding, but she was strangely disinterested in the fact. Her thoughts were concentrated on the fact that the rubble had settled in places in cement-like obstinacy so that it was impossible to prise some of it apart and quite impossible to think of a volume of water gurgling easily away through it.

It had taken a lot of effort to prise up enough rubble, and move it, to make one simple step-like little platform that was just wide enough and steady enough to take her weight. It felt, to her groping hands, a completely pathetic thing, and was exactly that in reality because it was barely nine inches high.

She stood there, recovering her breath, and added nine inches to her own height, wondering how long it would take for a deluge of rain, partly draining through rubble to fill and cover that height

It was like a problem of schooldays she thought in stifled amusement. If Miss X is five feet nine and is standing on a platform nine inches high, in a well whose diameter is Y inches, with a drainage capacity of A gallons an hour and a filling capacity of B . . . how long will it be before Miss X is dead 'cause waters closed above her head?

"Stop it!" she cried aloud, but her thoughts went on chanting the cruel little jingle till red light was abruptly gone, and the well and herself were in darkness.

$\bullet$ $\bullet$ $\bullet$

Useless to dwell on the fact he'd been wrong. Gabriel wasn't anywhere near the flat. She'd run right away, and he had to face it. He moved restlessly up and down the room. He'd thrown every window wide, but in a few moments they'd have to be closed again, he knew. The searing light was dying; thunder had given a few tentative rumbles in the far distance and the black cloud was spreading right across the sky.

As it had done Monday as Lisa Buchanan had reached the bridge. He could see her in his mind's eye, the dog loping at her side. The brute had howled, he remembered and suddenly he was wondering why Mark hadn't investigated the sound. The boy had been bored, if his story was true. Why hadn't he investigated the howling dog? He wasn't hurt, like Miss Traill. And what about the crying woman too? It would have told her people were about and might come to the houses. It would be natural for her to mop up and hurry away.

Who was she? Questioning her might help, or make things worse. Or leave them as they were now. But who was she? Who'd passed the houses, who might have seen her and could put a name to her?

The only name that was left from that Monday was Sherida Brown. But she'd gone over earlier. Still . . . had the woman been around then? Perhaps near the houses with someone else? A man? A man she'd quarreled with later, he thought hopefully. So that they'd parted—he'd gone off somewhere and she'd slipped into the houses for a quiet cry.

He went to the phone without stopping to wonder further, but when he heard her voice, when he put the question she simply sounded surprised . . . and faintly annoyed.

"Another woman? Columbus, the creek sounds as though it was drawing a circus crowd. There was someone in the houses right enough when I passed them because there was an old blue Volk outside one of them. Workman's car I'd guess and he probably hopped off right after I went by. He must have been the last of them to go or there'd have been other cars parked alongside."

"Yes, ' he agreed absently. But had it been a workman, or some-

154

one who'd been with the woman in the raincoat? Neither Mark nor Miss Traill had mentioned a car so it must have gone away after Sherida Brown had gone by.

He winced at the crash of thunder sounding again. He went to the windows, staring out at the dying red light, knowing a sudden aversion to staying inside. In a few more minutes he'd have to close the windows against the deluge, and then there'd be nothing to do but sit and stifle and think endlessly of Monday . . . and Gabriel.

So . . . go out? Go to the local, have dinner there, sit through the Saturday floor show perhaps . . .

Abruptly he slammed the windows shut, and in another minute was slamming the front door and running back to the car.

• • •

Sherida Brown leaned over the playpen, looked into the up-turned milky-blue eyes and said, "y'know what, kid? One of these days you're going to go grey worrying over problems, and they'll probably be all women, too . . . women in white and women in red and women in black and women in checks . . ." she scowled as the round features crumpled, snatching the baby up as the small mouth opened for the first yell. "Now what, now what? Oh, not again!" She patted with an expert, searching hand, muttered, "what a life! Why aren't kids able to use a sandbox like a kitten? I ask you! All right, all *right*!"

And Columbus, she thought impatiently, there were hardly any dry ones, and she'd left a full line outside . . .

She hefted the now bare-tailed child on to her left hip and made for the back door. "Look at it," she told him lightly, and winced as thunder sounded, frowned as the baby yelled in protest. The weather seemed all storms lately, she thought resentfully, throwing the door open, going out into the harsh red light. And the kid always yelled blue murder in them, too. Mum had moaned all Tuesday about her not getting back before the storm on Monday, leaving her to keep the kid's terrors in check . . .

She stopped still, her hand still holding the edge of the screen door.

She said, "Why, the bitch!" and was silent again, then whirled round, facing the door again, then stopped, as thunder crashed again. Come hell or high water or remembered things the nappies had to come off the line, she thought ruefully, and the baby put into a fresh one before he turned on the waterworks again, and five minutes, or ten, didn't much matter.

But when she lifted the phone, dialled Phillip Sturt's number, absently hushing the baby while her finger moved, there was only silence to answer her.

.   .   .

He'd done the right thing, he thought complacently. The dinner had been good, the pop singer not so revoltingly youthful and sway-hipped as usual; the comedian not so blue and so stale as normal for Saturday night. He looked at his watch, saw the hands nudging nine o'clock, and looked up, straight across the public bar, at Fred Zamia, in loud talk with two other men.

So Fred wasn't home, he reflected, and a jerk came at memory, reminding him that Eileen Zamia never missed what she called her "half-dollar's worth of life in the raw" at the Saturday evening cinema. He was on his feet as he remembered it, remembered laughing at the description, and was halfway to the phone box to call the Zamia house and try to get hold of Mark, when he remembered that it was impossible for Eileen to have her usual luxury. Not even Eileen's hide was rough enough to countenance her spending the first Saturday after her daughter's death in wallowing in cinema epics, even if Fred had sneaked off to the pub. Drowning his sorrows, Fred would have called it, he thought cynically.

So it would have to be the morning after all. He stood there, hesitating between going home and staying on. Few people knew him as Gabriel's cousin, so he didn't feel out of place, but the talk . . . always the running woman . . . was irritating. He'd go home, he

156

thought, but when he got to the door and saw the rain, he decided to stay on for a while longer at least.

.   .   .

Miss Traill cycled slowly into the street and saw at once that the house was in darkness. She'd been one of those who had gone while it was being built to admire and envy, but now, in the faint light from street lamps, with trees still dripping about it from the evening's deluge, it looked ugly—a vast hulking shadow amongst other shadows.

She wished, stepping off the bike, supporting her weight on the handlebars, that she hadn't bothered to come, but the constant non-reply had been a rising irritation she'd determined to cancel out by going to the house. She'd been sure that Gabriel Endicott would be in the place, simply refusing to answer calls or open her door, as she herself . . . she had remembered that in acute distaste . . . had done after being attacked by the Collins woman.

When the rain had abruptly stopped she had given way to the irritation and the need to talk, had flung on her plastic cape and put a scarf over her hair and stiffly, because of her knee, had cycled over, only to find now that the place was in darkness.

She wondered if the other woman was inside with the lights out simply to fool anyone who came poking round, but if that were so the door wouldn't be opened; and it was more likely, she thought impatiently, that Gabriel had gone into seclusion for the night somewhere else.

Reluctantly she mounted the cycle again, but still hesitated. There was still the clamouring need to tell what she'd remembered. She discarded the idea of Phillip Sturt as soon as she thought of him. He hadn't been on the pathway that Monday. She needed someone who'd passed down it towards the bridge, someone like Gabriel . . .

Mrs. Brown, she remembered.

She turned the cycle, began moving again, planning as she went, what she would say, wondering on the last of her journey, if again

157

she'd find a deserted house. But the Brown house was bright with lights and her ring was answered at once, but to her enquiry, given with an anxiety that surprised even herself, Les Brown looked merely impatient.

"Sherida? She's off at her mum's. The old lady got took crook. One of her asthma things. I was down at the pub and came home to cold chops on the table and a note to say she'd taken the kid and was spending the night down there. Anything important? You can have her mum's address if you like."

She shook her head mutely. The thought of a crowded household, Sherida harrassed, only half-listening between attending to her mother, and probably a squawling baby, as well as her younger brothers and sisters and father, was impossible.

"Righto then," he gave her a cocky grin. "If you'd care for a bit of grog and an hour with the telly tecs and me, come on in . . ."

She heard his soft laughter as she went down the path and was angrily resentful, then amused. He'd wanted to get rid of her, and had known his offer, and the half-leer, would send her away in disgust.

She mounted the cycle again, shrugging. There was always tomorrow, she reflected, as she turned towards home.

. . .

Carefully Gabriel lowered one foot, searched for the main layer of rubble, and stepped down. It wasn't the exhaustion of effort that made her lean then, quite unconscious of the water that was up to her waist, against the well wall. It was the exhaustion of sheer panic, of the strain of standing on the narrow ledge, while the rain poured down into the narrow shaft, soaking her hair round her face and her clothes round her body.

It had been impossible in that to feel the water banking up above her feet and legs, and too dark to see it. Only her hands, her slow careful lowering of her body, time after time, told her it was creeping up while the rain kept on, the noise of it magnified round and round in the confines of the shaft, and cold draughts of air swept down and over her, starting her teeth chattering uncontrollably.

But it was the driving wind that had saved her she was sure. The force of it had skimmed a lot of the rain straight over the shaft in a blinding, slanting deluge, so that the main force of water hadn't come down tumbling on top of her. Even when the rain stopped as abruptly as it had started, the wind was still there, and no longer drowned by the splash of the water, it was an eerie moaning round the shaft walls, while overhead it was driving the black clouds across the sky. She knew that because for fleeting seconds there'd be a break in the blackness, a greyness, a lighter patch, and once a star, then blackness again.

She knew the rain was going to start again. Soon. It would probably pour and stop and start and pour all over again all through the night, and each time more water was going to come down. She should, she knew, be bending, be scrabbling frantically, keeping her face from the water, while she scrabbled up rubble, built another step, and another . . .

Yet she didn't. She went on standing there, waiting hopefully for the water to start going down, start draining away. Her right hand was pressed to the exact place on her body where the water had come when she'd first stepped from her little pedestal. She went on standing, back against the well lining, looking upwards. After a little the light patter of a scurry of rain blew down the shaft on to her skin. Her other hand moved, feeling the one on her body, touching the water.

None of it had trickled away. Or else such a tiny amount had gone the surface line hadn't altered sufficiently to be marked.

She whispered to the sky, "Where *is* everybody? Why doesn't somebody come?" and her voice went echoing, ghostlike, with the moan of wind, up the shaft.

. . .

He stayed on till the last minute and then was reluctant to leave the circle of companionship and go back to the lonely flat. He knew he was hoping that a friendly hand might touch his arm and a friendly voice suggest the possibility of a card party.

But the hand that finally touched his shoulder was a policeman's.

He looked at the youthful face, wondering, as Gabriel had done before him, if the district only had men who looked barely above the age to be able to enter a hotel. He thought in anger that if they were older men they might have been doing something to protect Gabriel, instead of simply waiting for her to fall into their hands. He thought of her again in some lonely motel room, or scuttling among the shadows of the city night and he snapped, "What are you pestering me for?"

The hand fell away. The youthful voice said, "Where's Mrs. Endicott got to?"

When he gained no answer his voice sharpened. "Mr. Sturt, I'm asking you . . ."

"I heard. I thought you were leaving her alone until ten in the morning. You gave me . . ."

"There was a report of trouble up there. Some woman rang us and told us her daughter came home from the pony club with talk of children misbehaving up there; running round the house and trying to get in. The child reckoned she and another saw Mrs. Endicott racing out the back of the place and into the scrub. We've been up. The place is in darkness and there's no answer. A neighbour saw us and came to say you'd been up and were taking Mrs. Endicott away. Is that a fact?" The sharpness grew taut with irritation and impatience at the silence. "Have you taken her somewhere? Or has she bolted?"

He wasn't going to tell the truth, he knew. A lie wasn't going to help in the long run, because they'd have to know some time, and tomorrow, if not tonight, a police call would have to go out to find her. He still wanted her to have the night to think in. If she was cornered now she'd fight to such an extent they'd probably finish with the idea she'd deliberately held the wretched girl's head under water, but a night of loneliness, of time to think might bring her home, prepared with a sensible statement.

He was aware the young face was glaring at him, mouthing, "Mr. Sturt! I'm asking you . . ."

He snapped, "I heard you. You can hardly wait for me to answer and perhaps give you the chance to start chasing her across the country . . ."

"Don't be a fool." The admonishment came wearily. "Have you tucked her up in bed somewhere or not? That's all I'm interested in. Is she all right? If you haven't got her we'll send someone up to the old farmhouse at the back of Endicott's. If she was going through the scrub she could be planning to stay up there tonight—a nice hidey-hole sort of thing away from people. The place is still weathertight, as she probably knows, but I can't leave her up there."

At Phil's swift glance he shrugged, "Saturday night. The farm-house is a stopping-off place for the gangs of kids with nothing to do but drink and play up. They've about taken it over and if they find her there . . . well I just don't want any trouble. I've too much on my plate now.

"*Now* will you answer?" he pressed wearily. "Do you have her tucked up? Or do I send someone up to the farmhouse to scout round? If they chased her out in the dark she could break her neck in a rabbit hole—even," he smiled faintly, "fall down one of the old wells up there. Two of them around I believe though I've never seen . . ."

He was fighting down his anger and irritation at not being answered by the slow words, Phil knew, but abruptly they burst out in a tautly official, "Mr. Sturt, if you refuse to answer my question I'll have to take drastic action. You gave us an assurance that Mrs. Endicott . . ."

He said, and his own anger showed, "I haven't the devil's idea where she is! It's your own doing. Where was that man of yours when the children drove her out of the place? Running a two-up school in the scrub?"

The other retorted, poker-faced, "We were forced to call him in. This is Saturday night, Mr. Sturt. Some time you drop in to the station on Saturday night and see what we're up against. We thought she was O.K. Our man told us about that kid getting inside. We thought she'd never answer the door after that and she'd be set."

"Well she wasn't, but wherever she is she isn't anywhere near the farmhouse. Didn't you know the demolishers started on Friday—the bulldozers roared in at first light and it must have been nearly rubble when they knocked off. So she's nowhere near the place, and I can't see her staying in the scrub either, can you, to fall down a rabbit hole. She's in a motel somewhere, or has gone straight to the city."

CHAPTER SEVENTEEN

It was impossible, she thought helplessly. When she bent, fingers probing and tugging and pulling at pieces of rubble, she had to keep her chin raised and it was just above the level of the water. She didn't seem to be able to get any leverage to tug like that and twice pieces had come away so sharply that in her odd position she'd stumbled and had once gone straight backwards under the water.

The suffocating, cold chill of it had been terrifying. She'd lashed out furiously, struggling upright, having to take time to get her nerve and breath back before she started again and then, when she'd scrabbled up rubble, stood upright, waded carefully to her little platform to add to the new step of it she found that her wild lashing out had knocked against it and it was tumbled and fallen away.

If the rain had started at that point she knew she would have given up and simply stood there, quite helplessly, while the water rose up and up, but it didn't, and suddenly the cold air whistling in the well shaft was a blessing, because it made her move and start scrabbling and building again simply because it was far too cold to stand there and do nothing at all.

When the rain began again in another pouring deluge she had rebuilt her first step and added another, slightly larger. She stepped on to it hopefully, her face raised, feeling the strength of the downpour with her skin, deciding it was less than last time.

Then her foot slipped, the rubble under it rolled and her new step collapsed, her hands sliding frantically over the well lining, seeking a hold. Her torn fingers managed to find cracks and in another little while she eased herself upright again till she stood again on the first nine inches she had built, with the sound of falling water echoing round her in the shaft.

.   .   .

Fred Zamia must have been waiting in the shadows. When the policeman had gone he sidled up, said heavily, "Saw you in there, Phil."

When the younger man said nothing he added, "Tell y'what," and paused, picking at the pimple on his nose. "No one's said where Carol went. She flead Mark's eardrum after school Monday— told him to skip off, and not follow her. He only mooched to the creek later. But where'd Carol go to. Visiting, she told Mark, but no one mentioned a visit. And mind you, this Mrs. Brown gives out *she* went over early. What's to say she didn't get to the creek same time as Carol? Carol couldn't have made her visit 'cause no one's said they saw her and . . . what's to say she wasn't floating for a while. Then the water took her and your Gabriel sees her . . ." he lifted his suddenly coldly shrewd gaze, "Could have been Mrs. Brown gave her a smack. They loathed the sight of each other. If 'twas so, should be Mrs. Brown gets the blame."

There was silence while Phil pondered over it, wondering if the older man was going to offer to spread the story; throw Sherida Brown to the wolves; if he was paid enough? The thought was so sickening he recoiled from the other's flabby body.

But Zamia said only, "It's funny, no one saying. Eh? If she went visiting she couldn't have got there. Or the folks'd have said. Wouldn't they?" and then he turned and in a few steps was lost in the shadows of the street.

.   .   .

He sat for a long time in the car debating what to do. Go after Fred, corner him, ask him what he was getting at? Point out to him quite brutally that the idea didn't apply only to Sherida Brown, but to Mark himself? Go to the Zamia house and corner Mark? Question Sherida Brown? But she wasn't going to admit seeing the girl. And what about Gabriel? Why hadn't she told the truth in the beginning, instead of asking all over town all those questions about Bernice Strang's death?

He sat there, smoking, trying to place all those moving figures of Monday into the sunset landscape, placing one here, and then somewhere else; pinpointing time. Seeing Miss Traill first, because she was the one who must have come to the bridge and the houses first. He saw her glance at the sky and fall from the bike; saw her pick herself up and go off, hesitating at the houses, going inside, inspecting her knee.

And who'd come next? Mark and Carol he was convinced. Not Sherida Brown. She didn't come into it. It was Mark and Carol. The boy had followed the girl over the bridge just to find out where she was going, after she'd told him to leave her alone. And where the devil *had* she gone? Obviously the person must have been out. She'd turned round, found Mark on her trail and . . . yes, it all added up. Except, he thought wearily, for Gabriel's actions once the news was out. Mark and Carol, he thought again. The boy taunting the girl and the girl growing cranky. Perhaps she had thrown the first punch at him on the bridge. He'd punched back and run off and the girl had tried to follow; tried to wrench her foot free and gone . . .

But why hadn't she cried out?

She might have dropped like a stone, he answered that. Come up again with so much water in her mouth and lungs she'd been almost drowned already. It was an appalling thought. She'd been so close to help with Miss Traill in the houses, the boy on the path, Gabriel approaching.

But why had Gabriel afterwards asked all those questions about Bernice Strang?

He probed and pondered at that, and suddenly the solution was there. Had Carol gone to the Endicott house, been snubbed, and "got even" by writing an unpleasant, unsigned note to Gabriel telling her of that night?

That was it, he thought in triumph. It had to be. Because it cleared Gabriel. She'd seen the girl, run for help and had simply collapsed. The whole blame rested on Mark.

But how to prove it? The boy would never in a thousand years admit it, unless some sort of proof was thrust under his nose.

His mind went back restlessly probing through that sunset evening, seeing one figure after another, coming, going, falling, running. Miss Traill, Mark and Carol . . . the woman in the raincoat, he thought suddenly.

Why had she cried?

And who was she?

There was welling excitement in him now. Go back, he urged himself. Start again. See Miss Traill crossing, and entering the houses. Picture that. Now see Mark and Carol, the boy running off, laughing, jeering.

And the girl falling.

Had she come up again, managed to grasp the edge of the bridge.

And had someone followed in her steps?

The woman in the checked raincoat? Had *she* tried to help the girl and failed? Had she run then, in sick shock, sobbing and crying, to the houses?

And then . . . Gabriel had come, of course, he reflected in rising excitement.

The woman had looked up and seen her pass; thought, She'll get help. I can't face telling what happened. She'd seen Gabriel race away and had expected help to come.

So there it was. The whole wretched procession in the sunset. People hurrying through the evening . . .

But who was she? The woman in checks?

She'd been at the creek side afterwards. He didn't want to go to Mark—yet. He wanted to know the woman's name and see her first. So who else had been beside the creek when help had come? Lisa Buchanan had noticed no one. The police? He knew he didn't want to go to them either—yet.

So? who else? Miss Traill, he reflected. Human curiosity must have drawn her down to the site of the commotion. Perhaps she could put a name to someone else in the crowd; someone who could later pinpoint the woman in checks, because surely someone in the crowd had tried to comfort her tears.

It wasn't till he was nearly at the house that he thought of the time; reflected that she might well be in bed, but when he drove up the lights were blazing, and when she answered the ring it wasn't with indignation, annoyance, but with something that sounded like gratitude, relief, in her quick, "Come on in."

She led the way eagerly into the tiny living-room, swung round to face him, lips parted for speech, but he threw the question at her without waiting, saw surprise, then impatience in her face.

"My dear man, if I had seen anyone in the crowd I knew, would I have dared lie about the time I left the path? In any case everyone was so bundled up against the weather it would have been difficult to recognise anyone. That's why I lied. I was so sure if I'd been seen going home I looked such a draggled mess no one would have known me from Adam!"

Then she added, "Just the same, I can tell you who the woman in the checked raincoat is. No, don't interrupt!" She waved him to silence. There were two red circles in her pale cheeks. She said impatiently, "For heaven's sake sit down, man! It was after you left that I remembered. When I looked outside. It was just like that other evening. Exactly the same.

"So you see, I knew it was impossible!"

She looked at him triumphantly, then said, "But of course you don't understand. You weren't there. That's why I tried to get hold of Mrs. Endicott. She was there herself. She would have realised, when I explained, that of course she wasn't there at all. It was impossible! She had to be quite close up—she must know who the woman is."

Then she stopped. She pressed her hands over her mouth, closed her eyes a moment, then said briskly, "No, I'm not mad. It's simply that I've been bottling this up for hours." A quick wry smile touched her mouth. "It was just like removing a cork—all bubble, and no worth!

"Now let me start again . . . I went outside. I'd washed the spare bedroom curtains and hung them out this morning. I remembered the storm and went to get them. It was you talking of washing that reminded me. They're cream lace centre ones, and the side ones a grey damask with a silvery streak in them. Oh yes, this is quite pertinent. Don't fidget, man!" she snapped at him.

"But my back yard is long and narrow. From my back windows I was looking at the curtains from a distance. In that searing red light. And there on my clothes-line were pink lace curtains, and pinky-mauvy ones!

"You know, I really realised the storm light could have altered colours just after it all happened. That's why I thought of Mrs. Brown in her pale lemon dress. But I never realised just how wrong Mrs. Buchanan's story was.

"Don't you see things for yourself?" she asked impatiently. "She claims that even with that telescope she couldn't make out details. She didn't know what the woman's dress was like, or how she wore her hair, or anything. Except that the dress was white, and the hair was blonde.

"That's ridiculous! When she first saw the woman she'd have thought, 'There's a woman in pink'. She wouldn't actually have known if it was pink or white or cream or yellow or grey or anything else. She couldn't have! And as for the hair—that's impossible too! Blonde hair wouldn't have looked blonde in that light. It might have looked red. Or ginger perhaps. But not definitely blonde . . ."

He was back outside Lisa Buchanan's that evening, seeing the little dog rushing up the street—a dog that had changed from rosy-pink in the distance to a grubby white as it dashed by the car.

She was asking anxiously, "What did she wear that evening? Was it a checked raincoat? It must have been. Because she had to see that woman quite close up or she couldn't be positive of the white dress and the blonde hair. If she's positive of that she must have been close enough to make out a lot more than she's said. I'm sure she must have been in those houses; must have seen the woman run by.

"She must know who she is. But why has she lied all this time? What's she hiding?"

CHAPTER EIGHTEEN

She stood straight, face upturned to the sky where the clouds were wind-whipped so that she saw first only blackness, then greyness, then blackness again. The water was just above her breast, and it was a triumph—her own personal triumph—that it wasn't higher. She had remembered the discarded macintosh, scrabbled for it, forced her hands into the steady action of folding it over and over into a surprisingly thick pad that she had placed on her little pedestal before remounting it.

She even managed, standing so still, to gain a little humour from the fact that it was a convenience to have water so close to her chin. "I have merely," she told the well and the grey patch of sky above, "to lower my head and lap . . . like a cat . . . whenever I'm thirsty."

But she wasn't only thirsty. She was cold, and growing colder because there was no shelter from the wind and no avoiding the water. Her face was no colder than her body, but soon the whole length and breadth of her was going to be numb and cramped.

She wanted to move and told herself she had to move, to try and stave off the numbness and the coming of cramp, because if the latter came she wouldn't be able to stand upright, but she didn't dare move either. To step down off her pedestal of stone and padded macintosh would mean putting her face under water. To try and build another step up the well wall would mean her actually diving under the water; holding her breath, putting her face down, scrabbling up rubble, clutching it, drawing herself upright for another breath and going under again to place her dearly-won rubble on to the pedestal in the beginning of another step.

It was impossible, but she had to try it, because soon the rain might start again and . . . how long is a face? She pondered the question, between laughter and exhaustion. Seven inches? More?

Add that to length from chin to top of breast . . . then she thought, but the water has only to cover my mouth and nose . . .

She wrenched her mind away from it, strove for calmness again and a few more moments of respite before she need move. She concentrated on the sky, thinking again of Monday, of how red it had been, with the birds . . .

Cockatoos . . . silent for once, making for shelter. There were a lot round Larapinta. White cockatoos with yellow crests that had been that evening a cloud of rose pink flying across the sky.

I should have remembered it a long time ago, she thought bitterly. She wondered if anyone, seeing another sunset and a woman in white walking through it some time in the future would cry, "But how odd! She isn't a woman in white at all."

It was that thought, a determination to see Lisa Buchanan and make her tell the truth, that made her move.

.   .   .

Deliberately he turned the key, locking them into the staleness of the front room; locking out the blank, stunned face of Eileen; the angry thrust of Fred's flabby body.

It had been after eleven when he'd gone up the path, but the lights had still been on, a radio playing loudly somewhere inside. He had hardly bothered to explain what he wanted; said only, to Fred, "It's what you said to me tonight", and to the woman, "This is to save him from serious trouble," and had simply taken the boy's arm and marched him into the room.

He said, leaning against the door, "I want the truth. No nonsense. No evasions. No unnecessary cackle. Right?" He added, "No reward either, except a first-class belting if I catch you out in a single lie."

The upturned eyes were quite blank. For a heart-stopping moment he wondered if the boy were really simple—incapable of realising the difference between truth and falsehood, then he looked down, at the working hands, at the shuffling feet, and knew the youngster was numb with fright.

It seemed to take an unconscionable time. The boy at first persisted in saying over and over again that he hadn't meant any harm. Why should he, he asked plaintively, have thought to mention Lisa Buchanan had been in the houses, crying? She'd said she'd been to the creek. It had only been afterwards, when he'd been hearing nothing but Carrie's death all week, he thought it was funny she'd made it up about being at home and seeing the woman through a telescope.

He was quite sure, he insisted over and over again, that the woman wouldn't have had time to get home and back again, and home once more and back yet again before all the commotion started. She must have gone straight from the half-built houses to the creek and found Carrie at once. He was positive of it.

But no, he insisted, he hadn't seen or heard the running woman, or Gabriel either, except when she'd passed him before and he'd followed her to the first of the houses, and dodged inside. He'd later gone into one or two of the other places and finally he'd heard the woman crying. He hadn't wanted to be seen and be handed a telling off for being in the places and he'd hidden. Only later when he'd heard the move, the woman's steps crossing the bare planks, had he looked out and seen her, and it had been the dog he'd recognised more than the woman.

No, he denied, all that time he hadn't heard the dog utter a sound. Only later on had he heard it howling over and over. He would have gone to investigate, only the rain had been pouring down by then.

And no . . . and his denials were utterly convincing to Phil's ears . . . he hadn't been with his sister on the bridge. Certainly he'd gone to the creek, but he wouldn't have dared follow the girl. He hadn't the least idea where she'd gone, but he didn't dare follow. Carrie, he explained stolidly, had had a terrible temper and she was a lot bigger and stronger than himself. She'd have punched him, "well and good," his dulled eyes were defiant now. "An' I wouldn't have dared hit back. Carrie'd have gone straight to mum and I'd've got a belting. Mum always took Carrie's part. Carrie was mum's favourite. Mum nearly went crazy when she heard about Carrie. That was why I was sorry I told her about Mrs. Gabriel . . ."

Even the last words, Phil thought wearily, held complete conviction.

But why had Lisa Buchanan told that apparently senseless lie? Why involve Gabriel? Why not say, "This woman came rushing by, while I was in the houses," and describe her.

And then he thought, but Gabriel went to her, questioned her. Why didn't Mrs. Buchanan accuse her then?

He looked at his watch and was astonished; it hardly seemed possible that all the words, the urgings, the pressure on Mark, had been accomplished in little less than twenty minutes.

He asked urgently, "Mark, are you absolutely certain you don't know when Mrs. Buchanan came to the houses?"

The boy shook his head. He shuffled uneasily, his gaze darting all over the room. He said then, "I guess it was after Carrie must've fell."

"Why?"

The boy blinked. "She was crying."

"For Carrie you mean? But Mark, that's impossible," he pointed out impatiently. "If she knew Carrie was in the water why didn't she pull her out straight away . . . now wait!" he demanded urgently and after a moment asked, "You mean you think Mrs. Buchanan knocked her off the bridge? But Mark . . ."

The boy wasn't looking at him. He was shaking his head. He said rapidly, "I guess she saw . . . someone . . . hit Carrie and knock her over an' then well . . . the person'd kneel on the bridge, hmmm? Leaning to Carrie like? And it might seem like she was pushing Carrie under, not getting her out. And Mrs. Buchanan might've been scared and run an' then later she saw . . . this person . . . run away. And so she went back . . ."

All he could think of was that he had to get out of the room; out of the house. He felt suffocated, violently ill. He was asking himself if it was the product of a mind steeped in wild mystery stories . . . or truth?

He knew, quite certainly, that the boy could be right. Mrs. Buchanan might only have seen the person on the bridge from a distance and later . . . the woman could have had a handkerchief to her face.

But why hadn't she told everything? Why not say, "I saw this person push the girl, thrust her head under water . . ."

She hadn't been sure, he thought grimly. When she'd had time to think she couldn't be sure. So she'd spoken of the woman, spoken of seeing her from the ridge . . . hoping she could be wrong.

He thought grimly she must have feared she was right; must have grown more certain with every day of silence that followed.

The thing that mattered was what was going to happen to Gabriel now if Mark told his idea and Lisa Buchanan was forced to amend her story.

He knew he didn't want to go near the woman. If she was forced to speak out, there'd be no retracting her story later on. It meant that Gabriel had to get in first and tell a simple story of accident. Lisa, he was pretty sure, would welcome the chance of not being further involved and stay silent. Mark could be bribed into it, if necessary.

The urgent thing was to find Gabriel.

He smiled at that. It was funny to think the police had unwittingly told him where she was. He'd hoped, when he'd talked of the bulldozers, that the man wouldn't know it was a lie. He'd wanted Gabriel to have that night's quiet reflection and he hadn't been worried about her. The storm was a guarantee that even hoodlums wouldn't bother with a leaking farmhouse. Even if they did turn up she was safe enough.

He remembered the day last weekend when he'd been at Gabriel's and the temporary manager of Nick's firm had come up to tell her Endicott's had been given the auctioning of the farmhouse and land. The man had had new locks and bolts fitted, the windows shuttered and even the phone re-connected, ready for showing off to prospective purchasers.

He'd handed Gabriel a key and urged her to go up and have a look around before the auction was advertised. Whether she'd gone or not didn't matter. She had the key, and had, he was sure, remembered it as a hiding place. She wouldn't have come to himself . . . there was regret in that knowledge, in the remembrance of the hostility that had flowed between them at their

173

last meeting . . . so she'd gone to the farmhouse. And he'd known she was safe; that she could phone for help if it was ever needed.

He'd go up, he thought with relief. First he'd go home, get a torch to light the farmyard, and collect a raincoat. Even coffee. Something to drink while they talked. He'd go straight up after he'd collected the things.

. . .

The phone was ringing when he let himself into the flat. For a moment he was tempted to let it ring unheeded, and when he did answer, to hear Sherida Brown's impatient, "This was my very last try," he was simply irritated.

She rushed on, "Look, when you rang off before it was just going to storm. Same as Monday, when I looked out of sis's window and ran with her to get in the wash. Today baby squawled and I remembered his naps on the line and started off for them. And . . . they weren't white. Not from the back door. They were pink. And his little green dressing-gown was wine red, and his pale blue teddy was mauve."

They were suddenly both babbling at one another, then she said crisply, "I'll tell you something. That woman in the check coat was Lisa Buchanan. No, wait on—don't interrupt. I know, because of Carol talking and whining for more money. She wanted to buy a raincoat just like Mrs. B's. She told us about it. Les and self I mean. It was reversible. Checks one side and the other side was white."

"White?" he said dully.

"I've been thinking, what if it was *her*? She had it on white side out and hit Carol and bolted. Later on . . . well her yarn covered her, didn't it? If she changed the coat round and babbled about a woman in white anyone who'd seen the figure would never think of herself. Would they?"

When he didn't answer she said in annoyance, "Well, you did ask me about it all. I'm only trying to help. After all, according to you, she was bawling. What'd she have to bawl about, if it wasn't what she'd done?"

He continued standing there with the now silent phone still in his hand.

Possible?

Improbable?

But everything he'd thought of already had been both possible and improbable, it seemed now.

Where, too, had Gabriel come into it?

Had she honestly been telling the truth?

Had Mrs. Buchanan never seen her at all; never dreamed there was another woman in white about the place?

Possible?

Improbable? Whichever it was he had to see the woman at once.

He began dialling, the thought of the farmhouse and finding Gabriel gone under the greater urgency of speaking to Lisa Buchanan. He said into the phone, "I have to see you tonight. I know it's late. You see me, or you see me and the police."

．　．　．

It was humanly impossible. Quite impossible. She thought of later saying to Phil in excuse of her tears and trembling body, "It was impossible, Phil. I kept falling and going right under and twice I nearly didn't manage to get back on to my feet. I thought I was going to drown."

She thought then that perhaps she'd never talk to Phil about it at all. The water didn't seem to be draining away. She could see it just above her breast, the light shining on the surface.

Light? She looked upwards in astonishment. There weren't any clouds at all. They'd simply vanished. She was gazing at pin-pricks of stars in a sky that spoke of a moon somewhere unseen.

She knew it was deceptive—that another half hour and the blackness and rain might be back, but for the moment it was sheer pleasure to lean back and contemplate the tiny slivers of bright stars.

The first wave of cramp attacked her then.

175

CHAPTER NINETEEN

He could look into her ravaged face with no pity at all, because of Gabriel. He gazed at the face that had grown older and harder in the minutes they'd spoken and saw not it but a slim figure with dazed eyes, a trembling mouth and despairing, hostile voice.

He wondered how long she'd take to forgive him, remembered her saying she'd kept silent because she hadn't wanted to see suspicion and disbelief in his eyes, then Lisa Buchanan began repeating it all once more, as though, now she had finally spoken the truth she couldn't stop.

"She was a dreadful little girl. No, I am not ashamed of saying it. At first I tried to be friendly, then I could see into her morbid mind. I tried to send her away. She wouldn't go. I was cruel in the end, biting, sarcastic. I had to be, you understand? The way she was behaving was good for neither of us. She began to hate me though.

"Then on Monday we met. I'd been out with the dog in the scrubland the other side of the creek, letting him run and be free. No one saw us. No one was about. Finally I started back.

"She was coming across the bridge towards me. I think she had been on her way home, then saw me coming, and waited and came to meet me. A few minutes earlier, a few later—it might never have happened, I tell you!

"She stopped there on the bridge and said to me, 'I went up to your house. I waited a long time'. I said, 'You had no right there, Carol. I have told you to keep away from me. If this goes on I will have to tell your mother to spank you'. She laughed. She looked at me slyly in that horrible red light. It had just started then, I think. I do not really remember now. But that red light was on her face. She said, 'Mrs. Buchanan I've been reading a book. All about German war criminals. Do you know how a lot of them escaped punishment? They pretended to be victims. They

176

put tattooes like yours on their arms . . .' and she laughed again and said, 'but I guess you know pretty well, eh, Mrs. Buchanan'."

Her body seemed to writhe, become still again. She said wearily, "I knew what she intended—she was going to spread that horrible suggestion—whisper that I was really a monster from Germany's past, not a victim at all. I raised my hand without thinking and struck her. Violently. Across the face. It was unforgivable, of course.

"But I swear to you," she leaned forward in desperate pleading, "that she didn't fall. Don't you see, cannot you understand, that the dog would not have stayed silent. He would have barked hysterically. Surely that boy would have heard and come to see what was happening?

"The only sound Bruno made was a soft little growl when I hit her. She swung round with the force of the blow, her back to the unrailed side of the bridge, though I did not notice it then. And the heel of her shoe caught in the planks. She was furious. Her mouth started to open and I know I thought, 'She is going to swear. I can't bear it'. It seemed somehow the last straw, though I cannot expect you to understand.

"I simply ran. When I looked back she was still standing there. And then . . . she must, of course, have tried to wrench her foot free and come after me.

"But I swear to you, there was no sound when she fell. The water must have choked her. I do not think even that she fell for a few minutes—till we were some distance away, as there must have been a splash, and Bruno made no sound, did not stop and look back.

"Oh yes, the boy is right about my tears. I wept and wept. For myself and the past, and for a little child who could be so evil-tongued."

He could see tears now welling in the dark eyes. Then she shrugged.

"Yes, I cried. But what was the good of that? I wiped my eyes and looked from the frame of unglassed window in the house. And the light died. It was as though an electric light had filled the half-built room and had been switched off. I was so startled

I turned, expecting to see someone behind me. But of course there was no electricity, no other person. And when I turned back to the window great drops of rain began to fall.

"It was automatic, what I did then. I swear it. I had no reason then to think of protecting myself. I thought that she could have run by while I was crying, or even run to the ridge to lie in wait for me at my house. I actually hoped it would be the latter; that I could talk to her, soothe her, show her bluntly that I would call her story lies and make her appear very silly, if she dared to tell it.

"My eyes said to me it was raining; my ears said to me, thunder. My brain reminded me of my coat. When it rained I never wore it white side out. For some reason when the white was wet it became partly transparent, showing the other side in streaks and daubs. It looked most odd.

"What I did, changing it to the other side, was a simple automatic action. I had a scarf round my throat. I put that over my hair, called to Bruno and went.

"He saw her in the water and howled. Oh, how he howled! I dragged her out, did what I could, and fled. I never so much as considered the houses. I knew the workmen had gone. I never dreamt there was another soul in them," she said helplessly.

"I ran to the ridge. I passed two houses because I did not know if there was a phone and I did not dare waste time. I ran inside my own place, phoned, screamed to my neighbour to come, and ran back.

"All the time I thought only of Carol. Never of myself."

She drew a deep breath. "And then later . . . there is only that track from the town to the bridge. Just wide enough for one car. Work was to begin in a week or two on a two-lane road right along the creek, up to the ridge, and in front of it to join the main highway—from the bridge you have to walk nearly a mile, uphill, across scrubland, to the highway . . ." she shook her head. "But of course you know this. You must."

He nodded, but there was no impatience in him now. Only relief. A gladness. Because Gabriel was safe. Would never be in danger again.

He said, "Yes, I know. The running woman had to take the path. It wouldn't have been sane to run uphill, through a mile of scrub . . ."

She broke in, "The builder's lorries used that path. There were bitter complaints from cyclists and walkers. The path was all ruts. And when the ambulance came down it stalled halfway along and they couldn't move it.

"I remember one of the policemen crying to the crowd round Carol, 'Stir your stumps'. Such an absurd phrase. 'Stir your stumps, the whole mob of you,' he cried out. 'Get down the track and push it back or up here, so we can get the police car back down it with the girl'. Then someone rushed up and said a pressman's car had come rushing down the track, rounded a bend and crashed right into the back of the stalled ambulance.

"They radioed then from the police car to send a car or ambulance to the other side of the creek. One of the policemen told one of the men to run across the bridge and stop the car before we had more trouble. There is no creek path there, no houses—just a path going away from the bridge, up and away till it meets the road. But of course, you know. But the man was to run to the road and make the car driver back down the track to the bridge, as there was no space for it to turn down there.

"He ran halfway across and stopped and said, 'Her shoe's here —so that's what happened' and the policeman yelled out 'Don't touch that, man! It's evidence!'

"It was then I thought of myself. No one had questioned me. If they had I would probably have blurted everything out. But then, I began to think. Evidence, police, inquests . . .

"I wondered if Carol had already circulated that horrible lie, if people would say I'd done it deliberately. Oh, I was frightened —dreadfully frightened.

"The police took me home. They were kind. I played for time, thinking. And then . . . the phone rang. They told me she was dead. I thought only of myself then. I thought of saying I'd simply found her when I'd returned from my work, and then I thought again of that lie possibly circulating already.

"I thought—what if someone saw me run away? And so I told

179

the story of the woman in white. It accounted for her—it placed me up here when Carol fell. I thought," she said wearily, "it solved everything. How was I to know what would happen? What lies would start?"

She asked, "Do you think they will believe me now?" Then she shook her head, "But what does it matter. In the end it is nothing but a relief that it's over." She stood, asking, "Shall I come with you to the police? Or will you ring them and ask them to come here? Or . . . shall you go to your Gabriel first?" She sat down again, linking her hands in her lap. "I can wait. Don't you see, it doesn't matter that I should wait. Even when everyone knows I still have to live with it."

He wanted nothing so much as to get to Gabriel, but he didn't dare leave the woman. He didn't think she would try to bolt because she looked exhausted, but he was afraid she might recover, might regret what she'd told him, might even later deny it, or try to.

He said, "I'll ring the police."

.   .   .

She was becoming a complete Pollyanna, she thought wearily. First she could find something to be glad about in having water right under her chin, and now she was being glad about the cramps because desperation, the need to ease them, had found a way to exercise a little, and that helped to warm her a little, made her concentrate on working out other exercises and stifled thought about the hours ahead.

She could, she thought triumphantly, bend her knees, with back straight against the well wall till her chin touched the water, and then straighten. That was one thing. She could move her feet gently too, up and down, and use her hands, and arms. She was delighted with the variation of exercise she could do that way. She could stretch out sideways or in front of her as far as they'd go; she could shake her hands quite vigorously, and wriggle her fingers; put her arms straight above her head, bend her elbows and let fingers touch her shoulders.

The only thing was the exercises tired her terribly.

She thought suddenly, I want to go to sleep.

Panic was back. She wondered how long it would be before she fell asleep there on her feet and simply toppled into the water.

CHAPTER TWENTY

The policeman was staring at Lisa Buchanan as though he'd never really before noticed her, though when he'd entered the place he'd greeted her as somone well known.

He asked, almost suspiciously, as though he suspected some trick was being playing on him, "That's the truth?" When she nodded he said, "You'd best come to the station. Oh, you won't be there long, I should think. But we'll have to take some sort of preliminary statement." He stood up and said with more decision, "Yes, you'd both best come to the station."

Phil said shortly, "I must go to Gabriel."

The other's head jerked round. His gaze narrowed. "What's that? I thought she'd disappeared." He added in something that sounded like keen resentment, "I heard at the station she'd disappeared. Now you say . . ."

"I think she's at the old farmhouse at the back of the Endicott house," Phil broke in.

The resentment changed to real annoyance, "I heard at the station *that* was pulled down."

"Then you heard wrong. She ought to be there and I want to get to her without any further delay. Oh, to hell with your statement!" he burst out impatiently, "It's not *my* statement you want. It's Mrs. Buchanan's."

"*And* Mrs. Endicott's. You'd best go get her. That's right. You can get her and bring her down and . . . you say the old farmhouse?" he asked tautly. "That place is the party haunt of hoodlums. She wouldn't be up there. Not of a Saturday night. Why . . ."

"They couldn't get in." He explained why, but the man shook his head.

"You've taken too much of a chance. Oh, maybe the storm means they'll keep away, but that place is used by the car-strippers too.

Nice and quiet and out of the way. The boys take the cars up to work on them."

"She has the phone . . ." but in spite of the assurance of his words he was worried now. He wondered uneasily if she'd been driven further away still, or if she'd ever gone there.

The policeman was saying, "You'd best not go up there on your own, or in your own car come to that. I'll ring for someone to come and escort Mrs. Buchanan down, then we'll use the police car to go to the farm. On your own you might risk a knock on the head if you walk into someone." He shook his head, "But she won't be there."

· · ·

He said triumphantly, "Look there . . ." and the powerlights on the police car swept out over the scrub, pin-pointing scattering figures. "There you are!" He pulled the car round in a circle, shut off the engine and was out at once, "Car-strippers! Hey . . ."

Phil, stepping out the other side, knew a wild desire to laugh. It looked like an eager puppy trying to round up a gaggle of wily and experienced geese. There were only three figures he could see, but the way they were darting and circling they could have been three times as many.

There was complete farce in the running policeman with his waving arms and his outraged, "You just come back here!"

He didn't feel compelled to join in. The police, he thought grimly, leaning back against the side of the police car, had done nothing to help Gabriel. Let them solve their own problems. He'd done enough solving of problems to last him a lifetime.

He saw the policeman chase off after one of the figures that danced tantalisingly, jeeringly, just out of reach, and irritation at the absurdity of it made him start for the farmhouse itself.

The place was in darkness, but that didn't matter. Gabriel had possibly seen and heard the arrival of the cars in the dip some distance from the house. She would have switched off the lights in self-defence, to cower in darkness.

The thought of that sent him almost running out of the dip

183

and up the rise to the dark bulk against the now-moonlit sky and then stopped as a dark figure rose up out of the scrub right in front of him.

The boy was as startled as himself he realised. He gave a little yelp, spun round on his heel and darted away.

Phil merely shrugged, started up the rise again, hearing the boy crashing through the scrub, hearing the ghostlike cry that seemed to rise from the ground somewhere to his right.

"Help me, oh help me!" it cried through the night and seemed to echo, the repetition growing softer and softer, till it crashed out again as loudly as ever, "Help me, oh help me!"

He stopped, turning, knowing his skin was prickling in sheer fright. The sound was so horrifyingly ghost-like it kept him rooted there till the policeman came crashing back through the scrub, stopping panting at his side.

"Listen!" he said then, urgently, touching the man's arm, and the sound rose again. "One of them must have . . ."

The policeman laughed. "Bloody bastards," he said without rancour. "That's an old trick. One of them pretends he needs the last rites while the others get back to their car and get it started. He'll circle away and they'll pick him up further towards the road." As Phil took an uncertain step to the right he said impatiently, "Go down that way and you'll get your head knocked to keep you still till they're off. I'm not playing. You want to go to the house? We might as well. I can't catch them and they'll get out of the road while we're up there."

He turned towards the rise, and as the voice rose in ghost-like plea from the right he called back, "Help me, oh help me, mother dear, dear, dear!"

.   .   .

It was a car.

She was quite sure of it. The noise seemed to be caught by the wind and dropped down to her in the shaft, echoing round her.

She said, "I'm here," as though the people in the car would be searching for her. When she realised how absurd the idea was, and how soft her voice had been, she turned her face up, stretched out her neck and her whole body as though trying to get her voice closer and closer to the lip of the shaft so that it would bounce out, and rocket in its appeal through the whole outside world.

"Help me, oh help me!" her voice wailed up the shaft.

It seemed as though the well now wanted to be rid of her, because the shaft took her voice and magnified it and made it echo, so that each appeal cried out half a dozen times to the sky.

"Help me, oh help me!" she cried. Help me, oh help me, echoed the well.

. . . .

"Told you so."

The policeman was plainly pleased he'd been proved right, but Phil went on staring at the untouched padlocks over the heavy bolts and locks.

"Then where is she?" he demanded.

"In bed in some comfortable pub somewhere. Anyone who'd choose this old dump in preference to a pub would be blind crazy."

He said sharply, "She had no luggage. She couldn't have. I should have thought of that. She ran as soon as the children came. She wouldn't have had time to pack."

The policeman yawned, said patiently, "What's to say she hadn't packed before? She might have just been waiting the chance to skip. Look, we can't stay all night. I've got to get back to the station, and now I've got to report those hoodlums as well," he added morosely.

They walked down the rise in silence, then were abruptly still, listening.

Phil said sharply, "I thought you said . . ." His gaze swung down to the dip. The locked police car was still there, the power lights lighting up the scene like a film set. The half stripped car was there, too, but the other was gone. "They've gone," he said sharply.

The policeman's thick finger dug him in the ribs. "My aunt

Fanny they've gone," was the soft answer. "D'you know what they're going to do? Lead us through the scrub, jump us, bonk us and merrily strip *my* car!" Rage thickened his voice. "That's what they're going to do—*they* think. It happened to a mate of mine a while back. It won't happen to me. Come on. We're getting out."

He went running down into the dip, taking the car keys from his pocket. He called impatiently, "Want to stay all night?"

Resignedly he started for the car and the other man, then stopped. The moonlight was gone as abruptly as the red sunset had been wiped out hours before. Moisture touched his face and the policeman said disgustedly, "More rain!" holding open the off-side door for his passenger.

Phil took a step closer then stopped. He said shortly, "Wait a minute. Just one minute," and went running back through the now-driving rain.

He stood in it motionless at the spot where he'd heard the wailing cry, was turning away, satisfied, when it came again, repeating itself again and again. He went running back. He said shortly, "Get out! Get a torch. There's something radically wrong! You can't tell me hoodlums would stay on in this downpour to take a rise out of you. Move!"

He saw the rounded eyes and mouth, then half-tugged the reluctant man out, but once the policeman was moving he proved efficient and eager. Together they tracked the sound through the scrub. It was difficult to follow because it rose and fell and seemed hauntingly as though it was coming from deep underground at times.

It was the policeman who almost fell over the stone coping. He cried out, and as Phil came running, bending with the other man over the coping, the cry came again.

Torchlight flowed down the shaft, picking up the white upturned face, the sheen of water just below. The policeman said quite quietly, "There's rope in the boot of the car. Get it. I'll manage the rest."

None of them spoke. The two men didn't try to offer her comfort, Phil because he simply couldn't speak, the policeman because he was obviously intent on action, not speech. Gabriel herself was silent, watching the policeman's hands above her, coiling rope, knotting it. Then it snaked down, hitting the water in front of her with a little popping sound.

His voice called, "Take it, lift the noose and put it over your shoulders. Lift your arms through and up. Let the rope slide round your waist and hold it there. Can you?"

She said, "Yes."

It was so simple, the pull up so easy that it seemed incredible that a little time before she'd looked up at the darkened sky and told herself she'd never get out.

She said, with an almost childlike acceptance of a miracle, "Thank you. Thank you very much," and then Phil's arms were round her and he was talking. All the time he was carrying her to the car and wrapping her in the policeman's tunic and his own coat he was talking, telling her she was safe twice over.

ABOUT THE AUTHOR

Patricia Carlon was born in Wagga Wagga in 1927. She was educated at various schools in New South Wales before settling in Sydney. She continues to write, is a prize-winning cook, a keen gardener and lives surrounded by her cats.

She has written everything from articles, short stories and serials to short and long novels. Her work has been published in Australia and England under various names in daily papers, magazines and on radio. Much of her pseudonymous writing has been romantic fiction. Her most substantial work, however, encompasses crime and thriller novels, of which she has published at least fourteen. These were first published between 1961 and 1970 in England, mostly by Hodder and Stoughton in the King Crime series. Many have also been published in other European countries and her work has been translated into seven languages.

She was awarded Commonwealth Literary Fellowships in 1970 and 1973.

Her crime novels were not published in Australia, rejected in the sixties because publishers there, in her words, "didn't want anything but police procedure stuff."